DAYBREAK

DAYBREAK

The Days of Redemption Series, Book One

SHELLEY SHEPARD GRAY

**Doubleday Large Print
Home Library Edition**

AVON
INSPIRE

An Imprint of HarperCollinsPublishers

**This Large Print Book carries the
Seal of Approval of N.A.V.H.**

To Tom. Even after twenty-eight years, I still give thanks for you every day.

These shall wake the yawning maid;
She the door shall open—
Finding dew on garden glade
And the morning broken.

~from "Night and Day" by
Robert Louis Stevenson

Open my eyes that I may see wonderful
things . . .

Psalm 119:18 (NIV)

chapter one

The moment Viola Keim entered the main parlor of the Daybreak Retirement Home, she heard her favorite resident calling her name.

"Viola, come here quick," Mr. Swartz ordered. "I received another letter from Edward this mornin'."

After straightening her black apron over her purple dress and smoothing a wayward strand of hair under her white kapp, Viola grabbed a carafe of coffee, and did as he bid. She tried to summon a smile. Atle Swartz adored his son. Nothing could make his day like a letter from Edward.

Unfortunately, Viola could think of a dozen other things she'd rather do than listen to more news from the wayward Ed Swartz. She privately thought Ed sounded like a jerk.

Mr. Swartz's eyebrows clamped together as he glared at her. "What's wrong with your feet? You're walking so slow, you'd think they were cobbled together."

"I'm holding a pot of coffee, Mr. Swartz," she retorted. "I've no desire to spill it on the carpet or myself. Or you," she added with a small smile as she filled his coffee cup.

"It would be a real shame if I stained the carpet. Or burned someone," she said with a wink.

"You haven't burned me yet, Viola."

"There's still time. I've only been working here six months," she teased.

"Feels longer."

It did, indeed. Six short months ago, after a series of interviews, she'd gotten the job as an assistant at Daybreak, a retirement home for the Mennonite and Amish in the community. Right from the start she'd hit it off with the seventy-four-year-old gentleman. Though he was for the most part confined to a wheelchair, he had lots of energy and a biting wit. Somehow, he'd taken to teasing her, and she'd learned to give as good as she got.

Now she looked forward to visiting with him every day.

Though, truth be told, she didn't think he belonged there. He was too young to be in a retirement home. In her opinion, all Atle Swartz needed was someone to look out for him every once in a while. To do a little cleaning, and to make sure he had his coffee and supper.

Actually, what he really needed was his son. After all, it was a child's duty to look after his parents in their declining years. Not be off gallivanting in the wilds of Central America.

Not that it was any of her business.

Taking a seat beside him, she poured herself a cup of coffee as well and pretended she was eager to hear every word the illustrious Ed Swartz wrote. "I can't wait to hear what he has to say," she lied. "What a *wonderful-gut* way to start my day."

When Atle narrowed his eyes over the rim of his cup, she felt her cheeks heat. Perhaps she had laid things on a bit thick. "Is the *kaffi* all right?"

"*Jah*. It is fine. . . ." Carefully, he folded the letter smooth on the table in front of him. "Viola, are you certain you want to hear the letter? I'm beginning to get the feeling you don't enjoy them all that much."

Now she felt terrible. Sharing his only child's letters was the highlight of Atle's day, and she was ruining it by letting her personal feelings get in the way. "Of course I want to hear it, Mr. Swartz. I always enjoy sitting with you." Now that was the God's honest truth.

Two men sitting on a nearby couch cackled.

"You'd best watch it, Viola," one of them called out, his smile broad over a graying beard. "Atle's going to read every single word of Ed's letter. Might even read it twice, just to make sure you didn't miss a single thing. You won't be able to attend to anyone else for at least an hour."

"I guess I'll simply have to hope that you won't need me anytime soon, Mr. Showalter," she said sweetly, smiling when the men chuckled again.

The camaraderie she'd found with the residents of the retirement home brought joy to her heart. She loved working with the elderly folks in the area, loved feeling like she was making a difference in their lives.

"Girly, you ready to listen?" Two raps on the table with his knuckles brought her back to the present.

"Of course," she replied mildly. Truly, one day she was going to tell him that she was twenty-two years old. Too old to be called "Girly." "Ah, what does Edward have to say this time?"

After casting a sideways glance her way he cleared his throat and began. "Dear Daed, greetings from Nicaragua. As usual, the temperature is near ninety degrees, but my heart is warm from all the good works we've been doing. Not only have we given out a great amount of food and clothing lately, but we've also had some wonderful interactions with the children in the area. . . ."

As Mr. Swartz continued to read about Ed and his mission work, Viola tried to imagine what would possess a man to leave everything he knew and loved to attend to people so far away. Though of course he was doing many good things with the Christian Aid Ministries Association, there was much in Holmes County, Ohio, that he could focus on.

Most especially, his wonderful father.

As Atle continued to read, stopping every now and then to repeat what his son said—just to make sure Viola didn't miss a single word—she felt her attention drift. Edward's stories, while impressive and heartfelt, simply didn't mean that much to her. Not when she had plenty of concerns right here in Berlin.

She couldn't imagine walking away from her family, it was so tight-knit and demanding. At home, she was surrounded by all things familiar, and found comfort embracing traditions that had continued for many generations. Though her family was New Order Amish, not Old Order like many of the other Amish in the area, or Mennonite like some of the residents of the home, she'd found that her traditions and values weren't any different from the folks she helped.

She was grateful for the many blessings God had graced her with. She'd grown up in a beautiful white house, part of the newest addition to their already sprawling property that had first been built in the 1920s.

She was close to her grandparents, who lived in the *dawdi haus* behind them, and close to her parents, and to the few of her aunts and uncles who hadn't moved far away.

She'd always gotten along fine with her brother Roman and her twin sister Elsie as well.

Of course, things would likely start changing soon. After all, she and her siblings were all of marriageable age. One day, she and Roman would get married and move on.

But no matter what happened, she intended to live close and continue to help Elsie. Her sister was always going to need a lot of help. Born with a degenerative eye disease, Elsie would need at least one of her siblings to look out for her for the rest of her life.

Just imagining the idea of leaving Elsie in the care of strangers made her heart clench.

Thank goodness neither she nor Roman was like Ed Swartz!

". . . and so, Daed, I must let you go. The children are about to open their shoe boxes and I don't want to miss a minute."

That caught her attention. "Shoe boxes?" she blurted. "Why in the world does he need to hurry to open a shoe box?"

"It was Christmas, Viola," Atle said with more than a touch of exaggerated patience. "Weren't you listening?"

Oh!

"There's only one right answer, Viola!" Mr. Showalter called out. "Otherwise, you'll be hearing that there letter again, mark my words."

After giving her heckler a disapproving frown, she got to her feet. "Of course I was listening, Mr. Swartz. Once again, your son Edward seems to be having a mighty fulfilling and charitable life. I just was caught off guard by the mention of the shoe boxes. That's all."

But Atle didn't buy her words for even a minute. "It was Christmas, Girly. This was his Christmas letter. Those boxes were from us! Our shoe-box ministry! Don'tcha remember?"

"Sorry. I had forgotten."

"I didn't."

With more patience than her parents would have ever guessed she had, she smiled tightly. "I'm sorry, Mr. Swartz. It's simply that, uh, I thought he would have been talking about something else by now. It is the middle of January, you know."

"He's far away. All the way in Nicaragua," he said slowly. Pulling out the country's name like she had trouble understanding things. "The letters take a long time to get here."

Feeling her cheeks heat all over again, she tucked her chin. "Oh. *Jah.* I mean, yes, of course. Thank you for reading it to me."

"But don't you want to talk about the note? I'm sure you have questions. . . ."

The only question she ever had was "why?" As in *why* did Ed never ask his father how he was doing? As in *why* didn't he ever come back to visit? *Why* didn't he care enough to stay close to home?

But of course it was best to keep those things to herself. She didn't want to hurt Mr. Swartz's feelings. "The letter was so thoughtful, so detailed . . . I, um, I don't have a single question. And I had better deliver more of this coffee before it all runs cold. You know that Mrs. Ames expects me to visit with several people this morning. Have a good day, now."

The spark in his blue eyes faded. "You're

certain you can't stay for a bit longer? I have some more news to share."

Oh, he was lonely. It broke her heart. "I'm so sorry, I can't stay today." She just wasn't up to hearing one more story about his perfect child. "I've got quite a bit to do before I leave this afternoon."

"Well, all right, then. Have a good day, Viola."

"You too, Mr. Swartz."

After topping off his cup, and refilling the other two men's mugs, she rushed out of the room and went to the kitchen, where she put coffee and snacks on a tray for the ladies in the craft room. Balancing too much on the white wooden tray, she hurried out of the kitchen, turned left, and then headed toward the back of the building.

When two cups started to wobble, she abruptly stopped and set them to rights. Then rushed forward, and promptly ran into a man leaving the office.

When their bodies collided, the plastic bowls of snack mix fell to the ground. And the coffee carafe began to wobble.

"Watch out!" she said as she tried to gain control of the tray.

Two capable-looking hands reached out

and pulled the tray from her. "Careful," he murmured, his voice deep and steady. Almost as steady and strong as his hands looked. "You almost ended up wearing that coffee."

Feeling a true mixture of relief and embarrassment, she looked up into the speaker's eyes.

And noticed that his dark blue eyes were tinged with gold. Much like a certain older gentleman's. "Oh!" she gasped.

"What?"

"You . . . You look much like one of our residents."

"Atle Swartz?"

"Yes. Are you a relation?"

"You could say that. I'm Edward Swartz."

If his unusual eyes hadn't given him away, his tan and square jaw would have. The man looked like a carbon copy of his father. Well, a younger, spryer, tanner version of him.

"You finally came back?" she blurted before she could stop herself.

"Finally?"

She bit her lip as her director, Mrs. Ames, came out of her office. "Is everything all right, Viola?"

"Oh, *jah.*"

Mrs. Ames stared at the tray the man was holding. "Any reason Ed here is holding the coffee tray?"

"*Nee.*" With a jerk, she pulled the tray from his hands. "*Danke.* Um. Excuse me, I have work to do."

"Hey, I'll be happy to help you," he said after the administrator turned to the right and walked down the hall. Leaving the two of them alone again. "That tray is fairly heavy."

"I can manage just fine." Unable to stop herself, she raised a brow. "Besides, don't you think it's time you went to see your father?"

She turned without waiting for an answer.

But still, her cheeks burned with shame for her behavior. And for the fact that as much as she didn't like him . . . she couldn't help but notice he was far more handsome than she'd ever imagined.

Ed Swartz stood in the middle of the black-and-white-tiled hallway, more than a little perturbed. First, that woman almost spilled coffee on him, then acted like he was about to attack her while he helped her with the tray. . . .

Then had reprimanded him. Like he was a wayward child.

What was her problem? Was she just in a bad mood, or had she really gotten upset that he'd knocked into her?

Maybe he was simply used to the kindness of the people he worked with in Nicaragua. The people there had so little, they were thankful for the smallest amount of care or consideration.

"Can I help you, young man?"

An elderly lady wearing tan polyester slacks, white tennis shoes, and a bright blue sweater pointed to the sign-in sheet. "If you're visiting, you've got to sign in. It's the rules."

"Sorry. I guess I got distracted." After signing his name, he said, "Can you tell me where I might find Atle Swartz?"

A wave of emotion transformed her face. "Are you his son?"

"Yes, ma'am. Edward."

"All the way from your mission trip? Praise God!"

She darted around the welcome desk, squeezed his arm, and practically dragged him down the hall. "Your father is going to be so happy to see you!"

He doubted his father's happiness would hold a candle to his own. He'd missed his father terribly during his two-year absence.

But his steps slowed when he caught sight of him, sitting in his wheelchair in front of the gas-lit fireplace. His father looked older, frailer.

"Daed?"

His father's head popped up. Stared at him like he'd risen from the dead. "Edward? Edward!"

As Ed crossed the room and wrapped his father in a hug, he realized nothing else needed to be said. For now, they were together, and nothing else mattered. With effort, he pushed all thoughts of the woman with the pretty brown eyes from his mind.

In the grand scheme of things, she didn't matter to him at all.

Peter Keim pulled another cardboard box off a shelf, looked at his mother, and groaned. "Mamm, every time I turn around, I'm finding another box of yours. Why do you have so much stuff?" And more to the point, how come he hadn't seen any of it before?

It was like his mother had hidden a secret life up in the rafters of their home, and it had all gathered dust and begun to slowly rot. When a spider crept out from under the box's top flap, he grimaced. "We should throw this all out."

From the other side of the attic, his mother looked at the four boxes, two trunks, and six or seven large wicker baskets that were filled to overflowing. She looked a bit surprised to see everything, but even in the dim light of the attic, Peter noticed a faint gleam of anticipation, too. "Oh, Peter, settle down. It's not so much stuff. Not really so much for a woman's whole life. I am fairly old, you know."

Peter sighed. His mother had been talking like that for months now, which was exasperating, since she was only sixty-four and enjoying exceptionally good health. As far as the family was concerned, the matriarch of their family had decades to go before she went around proclaiming she was old.

"Well, all this cleaning is making me feel old," he said. Opening up one of the five green plastic garbage bags he'd brought up to the attic, he crouched down next to one of the trunks. "This women's work is wearing me out."

As he knew she would, his daughter Elsie found fault with that. "Father, you mustn't talk like that. Cleaning is most definitely not only women's work. Besides, you know Mamm with her asthma can't be up here in all this dust."

He did love how prim and proper his daughter was. "I'm just teasing, Elsie. I don't mind helping with the attic. Besides, it's a whole lot warmer up here in the attic than outside in the fields."

She rubbed her arms. "I'm tired of winter and it's only January."

"Patience, Elsie," his mother cautioned. "Everything comes in its own time. Even spring."

Getting back on track, Peter brushed aside yet another traveling insect and pushed the box he'd just taken down a little more toward the center of the attic. "I can't wait to see what you have in here. This doesn't look like it's been touched since you moved in."

Before his eyes, his mother stiffened. "I had forgotten that box was in here."

"Then it's time we found out all your secrets," Elsie teased from her chair near the window. "Mommi, you know what's going to have to happen, don't you? You're going to have to tell us all the stories that go with the items in the box."

For some reason, his mother looked even more perturbed. "I doubt you'd be interested, Elsie. There's nothing out of the ordinary inside. Nothing that you haven't heard about at least a dozen times. You know, dear, perhaps you should go downstairs with your father. I'll finish up here on my own."

"I'm not going to let you be up here by yourself, Mamm," he said. "Stop worrying so much."

"And I'm not going to leave you, either, Mommi. There might be something inside that you've forgotten about. . . . A deep, dark secret . . ."

His mother laughed. "I think not. My life isn't filled with secrets. That's not what the Lord intended."

Peter felt his smile falter as his mother's

pious remarks floated over him. For all his life, both of his parents had set themselves up as pillars of the community. And as models for their six children to follow.

But their markers were so high, their children never felt they could meet their parents' high standards. It was one of the reasons his brothers Jacob and Aden had moved to Indiana, and his little sister Sara had moved all the way to New York.

Even though he was the middle child, not the eldest son, he was the one who'd elected to live with his parents and take over the running of the farm. It made the most sense. He was used to keeping the peace—a quality that was definitely needed in his parents' company.

But even he was finding it difficult to hear their criticisms day after day.

Well, at least that was the reason he gave for his own private behavior.

Pushing his dark thoughts away, he opened the flaps of the box and pulled an armful of the contents out. On top was an embroidered sampler.

"What does it say, Daed?" Elsie asked, reminding him that with her eye disease, it was getting harder and harder for her to see most anything.

"It says 'Start and End the Day with Prayer.'"

Elsie smiled. "That sounds like Mommi."

Indeed it did. Lovina Keim was the epitome of a dutiful Amish wife. She'd borne six children, had organized charity events for the community, kept a bountiful garden, quilted well, and could still outcook most women in the area.

She was a handsome woman, with dark brown eyes, which her children and grandchildren had all inherited. She was a hard worker and never asked anyone to do anything she wasn't prepared to do herself.

However, she was also critical and judgmental. It was next to impossible to live up to her expectations.

Elsie moved closer, kneeling next to him. "What else is inside?"

Peter looked at his mother, who seemed frozen, her eyes fastened on the box.

Slowly, he pulled out a heavily embroidered linen tablecloth, and a pair of crystal candlesticks. Peter shook his head. While some Amish women did buy some pretty tableware every now and then, these items were extravagant. Even more, he'd never seen them before. "Mother, where did these come from?" He held up one of the heavy candlesticks.

That seemed to set her back into motion. Busily smoothing out the rough fabric of a quilt, his mother glanced away. "I'm not sure. I've forgotten."

Peter had never known his mother to forget a thing. "Come on, now. You must have an idea."

"I do not. If I knew, I would tell you, Peter." Standing up, her mother shook her head. "I'm getting tired. I no longer care to look in these boxes." Her voice turning pinched, she continued. "Elsie, please walk with me back to my rooms?"

Obediently, Elsie moved to stand up, but Peter held her back with a hand on her arm. "*Nee,* stay, Elsie. Now that we've started digging in here, I'd like to see what else is inside." Something was propelling him forward. Maybe it was his mother's unfamiliar hesitancy.

Perhaps it was his own selfish wants—a part of him enjoyed seeing her discomfort. It gave her a taste of what he'd felt much of his life. With purposeful motions, he pulled out another sampler of a Psalm, the stitching uneven and childlike. A cloth doll. An old packet of flower seeds.

And then a framed photograph, wrapped in plastic bubble wrap. The Amish didn't accept photographs, believing that copying their image was a graven sin. "Mamm, what in the world?"

"Peter, don't unwrap that."

His mother's voice was like steel, but Peter ignored the command. He was forty-two years old, not fourteen. And now he was curious.

"Who is this, Mother?" he asked as he pulled the plastic away, finding himself staring at a photograph of a beautiful young woman. Her hair was dark and smooth, her eyes the same coffee-with-cream brown color that looked back at him in the mirror.

A vague thread of apprehension coursed through him.

"Who is it?" Elsie asked.

"It's a woman, a woman of about your age," he said patiently, ignoring the tension reverberating from his mother. "She's mighty pretty, with brown wide-set eyes and hair. Why, she could be your twin, Elsie."

Elsie gazed at the photograph, but the three of them knew it was basically for show. Her eyesight had gotten much worse over the last two years. "She is pretty," she allowed. "Though we all know I already have a twin. I'm glad this girl isn't one, too. I have no need for one more!"

"Since she's an *Englisher*, she couldn't be your twin. Ain't so, Mamm?" He chuckled, raising his eyes to share a smile with his mother. Then stilled.

His mother looked like a deer caught in the headlights of an oncoming vehicle. Her face was pale, twin splotches of color decorating her cheeks. And her eyes . . .

They were the exact ones in the photograph.

Suddenly, he knew. "Mother, this is you, isn't it? This is you in a cap and gown. At your high school graduation."

His mother averted her eyes.

Elsie gasped. "Mommi? What were you doing, dressed up like an *Englischer*?"

Though his mother said nothing, Peter realized he didn't need an explanation. The item in his hands was clear enough. Slowly, he got to his feet, his knees creaking with the effort. "Your grandmother wasn't dressed up as an *Englischer,* Elsie," he said quietly. "For some reason, she wasn't Amish here. She was English."

Bitterness coursed through him as he thought of the many, many times she'd be- littled all of them because they weren't perfect enough. Weren't devout enough. Didn't obey the Ordnung to the letter.

The way her criticisms had driven his siblings Jacob and Aden and Sara away.

The way her perfection had made his other brother, Sam, try too hard, had made his youngest sister, Lorene, feel terrible about herself.

The way her iron will had even pulled apart his God-given easygoing nature, causing him to do things he shouldn't.

And she'd done all of this on top of a heap of lies.

He thought of all the times she'd even been critical of his sweet wife, Marie. The way she'd criticized meals and house- keeping and sewing.

Appalled, he stared at his mother. Really looked at her, as if for the very first time. "Talk to me, Mamm. Were you raised English?"

"Yes."

"Were you ever going to tell us the truth?"

For a few seconds, time seemed to stand still. The dust particles in the air froze. Then Lovina Keim's face turned colder. "*Nee.*" Slowly, she walked to the narrow, steep steps and began descending.

Still holding the photograph in his hands, Peter let her walk down by herself.

"Daed, what does this mean?" Elsie asked.

It meant everything. But of course, he could withhold the truth as well as his mother.

"I don't know," he whispered. "Let's go downstairs, too, Elsie."

Slipping the photograph under his arm, he helped guide Elsie down the stairs.

When she was in her room, and he was sure the rest of the house was silent, he strode to his bedroom, opened up the door to his bedside table, and pushed aside the neat stack of books.

Behind the well-worn hardbacks, he found what he was looking for.

And though it wouldn't solve his problems, it would help him not care. Even if it was just for a little while.

chapter two

It seemed that two years could, in some ways, feel like a lifetime. After their lengthy hug, Ed stepped back and took a closer look at his father.

When he was growing up, most folks said he was a carbon copy of his dad. They both were blessed with hair so dark it seemed inky black and deep blue and gold eyes. The unusual combination had been a source of pride for Ed growing up. More than one girl had commented on his looks.

But he'd always been happier to know that he was following in his father's footsteps. There was no better man in the world. Now, after two years' absence, he realized that he was looking at his future.

Yes, Atle Swartz still favored blue shirts, black trousers, and black suspenders. He still had his gray beard, too.

Of course.

But other things were different. His father looked smaller and frailer than Ed remembered. Whereas Ed used to have to struggle to carry as much hay as his father, now his *daed* looked like he wouldn't even be able to push a wheelbarrow. His body looked half its former size. His father's hands, once so strong and perpetually suntanned, now looked heavily blue-veined and pale. Especially here, under the fluorescent lights of the card room.

"Seeing you does my heart good, Edward," he said.

Feeling tears prick his eyes, Ed grabbed a chair and sat across from him, so close their knees were touching. "It's been too long, Daed." He ached to say he was sorry for his absence, but he wasn't sure if that was true. He'd missed his father, but his heart had been full of the joy he'd received from the people of Nicaragua. Doing mission work had changed him in many good ways. And because of that, he couldn't ever think of his time in Central America as a mistake.

"It has been too long," he agreed, his voice hoarse with emotion. "I am *verra* pleased to see you. And shocked, too!"

"But it's a good surprise, yes?"

"It's good . . . but confusing, too." His eyes narrowing, his *daed* looked him up and down. Just like he was checking for new flaws. "You must tell me what you are doing here."

"I'm seeing you, of course."

"Don't tease." Pointing to a sheet of notebook paper on the table, his father said, "I received your letter this morning. You gave no indication that you were on your way home. I think you could have done that, son." He paused, looking him over yet again. "Unless . . . something bad happened?"

"Nothing bad happened." Eager to push off any more charges of misbehavior, Ed picked up the note, saw the date, and grinned. "This letter is dated three weeks ago. I've written you at least two more letters since then."

"But surely you could have remembered

to let me know you'd soon be heading this way . . ."

Knowing his father had no concept of how disorganized life at a mission post could be, Ed tried to explain things as well as possible. "Daed, when I wrote this, I didn't know I would have to leave so soon."

"You had to leave quickly?" Worry flashed through his cloudy eyes. "What happened?"

Aware that several other residents of the retirement home had crowded around, Ed took time to weigh his words before answering. "Nothing terribly exciting. The folks at the home office took another look at the staffing at all of their sites. Some locations needed more people, other sites had too many. They had to make some cuts, so a few people were sent to Africa, others home."

"That doesn't sound like any way to run a company."

Knowing better than to try to explain the delicate balance CAMA—the Christian Aid Ministry Association—had to ensure was kept in each country, and the amount of work it took to provide for the many people they served, Ed shrugged and went for the simplest of explanations. "The people in charge were told that they had too many Americans in the compound. Next thing I knew, they were telling me I was on the list to leave."

"I hope you weren't in trouble." His father's gaze searched his own, the same way he used to look him over when Ed would come home from school early.

Luckily, he had a lot of practice deflecting his concern. "Daed, stop looking so worried! And why would you think I'd be in trouble? I was on the list because I'd been there the longest. Sending me home was their way of rewarding me for my hard work."

"I suppose that makes sense."

Ed didn't know if it did or not—all he knew was that he hadn't needed any kind of reward. Long ago, he'd learned to put his needs far behind the needs of the people he'd been serving. No matter how much he was inconvenienced or shuffled around, it wouldn't hold a candle to the difficulties the people he was serving went through each day. The people he'd come to care for. He loved his mission work, but he had to admit, it was nice to be back in

Ohio. At the moment, he was grateful for the cold air and was looking forward to a comfortable bed.

And nothing was better than sitting with his father. "Daed, honestly, I was glad they asked me to leave. I'd been there almost two years. I was ready to come home for a spell."

"And I am glad you're here, too. Now, how long will you be staying?"

"At least six months."

Some of the light in his father's eyes faded. "And then you'll be off to somewhere else?"

"That's the plan."

"Ah."

That one word cut through him like a knife. And with that cut, Ed felt the guilt that sometimes threatened to swallow him whole in the middle of the night. Since his *mamm* had passed away almost three years ago, it had been only him and his *daed*. Now it was hardly even that. Though they'd had countless conversations about his calling to mission work, Ed hadn't left the country without a certain amount of remorse.

No matter what his *daed* said to the

contrary, Ed couldn't help but wonder if moving his father to the retirement home before he'd left was the right choice.

But there would be time enough to go over plans in the next few days and weeks. And for sure, time enough to rehash his father's living arrangements. "What's new with you here?"

"Oh, nothing much. I've been beating Jacob Showalter here in cards almost every day, and I heard from your cousins in Indiana—two of them have new babies. And we have a new worker here . . . Viola Keim."

Hearing her name was jarring, like a barrel of dishwater had just been tossed on his head. "I saw Viola when I arrived."

His father's gaze softened. "She's a right pretty thing, ain't so?"

He would have liked to say he hadn't noticed. But he had. Few women could carry brown eyes and brown hair so well.

It was a shame she was so full of herself. "She is pretty." For what that was worth. Pleasing looks were well and good, but if they didn't match a sweet personality, he didn't think they counted for much. "Who else have you been visiting with?"

But his father wasn't about to be side-tracked. "That Viola is a dear girl. I've been reading her your letters. Every one."

"Every one?"

"Oh, *jah*. Sometimes, multiple times."

Ed felt his cheeks heat. He'd written some of those letters late at night, when he was so tired and exhausted that he'd given in to temptation and written more about his feelings of loneliness or frustration or diffi-culties than he usually would. He'd often treated the letters like journal entries—so much so that he'd often considered not sending them to his father for fear that it all would be too much for him to handle.

Realizing that all of his private feelings had been read out loud was embarrass-ing. He recalled one letter where all he wrote about was how he wanted a truly hot shower!

"Daed . . . I hadn't intended for you to share the letters."

"But you had to know I would."

"I guess I did," he said weakly. Now that he was sitting here with his father, he real-ized he'd naively assumed his father would feel as protective of the letters as Ed had.

But most of all, he'd not imagined that

he'd be sharing every bumbling word he'd written. And not to beautiful volunteers!

"Oh, Viola enjoyed them. I know she did. Why, I think she could be interested in you. You should see if she wants to go walking or something."

Ed was pretty sure that the only place Viola would want to walk was away from him! "Daed, I don't think so."

"But she's your age. She'll make someone a fine *frau,* mark my words."

It was time to nip this in the bud. "Daed, I didn't come here to go courting. I want to spend time with you."

"Well, that should take up one or two hours a day. What are you going to do with the rest of your time?"

He laughed, though it was uncomfortable. "I thought we could do some things together. Maybe go on a trip." As his guilt crept forward he added, "Maybe you want to live at home while I'm back? I'd enjoy that."

"You want me to sit by myself in that big *haus* while the two of us try to put together some terrible meals?"

Put that way, it did sound kind of ridiculous. "I can cook. Some." Actually, he'd gotten pretty good at making rice and beans.

His father scowled. "I have no intention of eating your cooking."

"I don't cook that badly."

"I'm sure it wouldn't compare to the food here."

He didn't know why his feelings were hurt, but the criticism did sting. "Hey, now, Daed—"

"Besides, this is my home now." Patting the thick cushion of his chair, he cast Ed a self-satisfied smile. "It took me a bit to get settled in, but now that I am, I'm in no hurry to go anywhere. Surely you can understand that?"

"I guess that makes sense."

"It makes perfect sense."

While he'd been gone, Ed had been thankful for the retirement home. He was glad his father had friends, and was in a place where so many eyes could watch out for him. But he'd never believed that his father would think of it as his living preference. "So, have you been to the house recently?"

"Nope. I haven't been by there in months. I've been paying someone to look after it."

That surprised him. What also surprised Ed was his own uneasiness about being back home and staying there by himself. He knew it would feel emptier than ever without his father there.

And he'd be forced to deal with all the memories of his mother, too.

"Daed, how about we go by there this afternoon? We could take a look around, pick up some groceries. Maybe even make soup and sandwiches like we used to."

His father's brow wrinkled. "I don't think so. We're going to have sundaes at four."

Now he was getting irritated. Honestly, his father was acting as if he'd intruded upon his life! "I can take you out for ice cream."

"It's near on thirty degrees out, son. Why would I want to leave the comfort of the fireplace if I don't have to?"

How many times had his father come in from the cold with red cheeks and a broad smile? Ed was flooded with memories of his father working outside for hours, no matter what the temperature.

Making him realize again that they'd both changed considerably while he'd been away. "I could make you a fire at home. . . ."

"*Nee,* Edward." As if he noticed his dismay, his father softened his tone. "Listen, I am glad you're here. I am. It's a blessing to see you, and I give thanks to God that you are in such good health and spirits. If you'd like to stay here and have ice cream, that would make me happy. But I'm not leaving this building."

There was only one right reply, but to his surprise, it came out a little sharp. "Ah. Well, all right."

"*Gut.* Now go get yourself some *kaffi,* then you can sit with us and tell us all about your adventures in Nicaragua."

Ed was perfectly happy to do that. Actually, the whole way home, he'd thought of nothing but telling his father all about the kids and the people, and the lush beauty of the area.

But now all he could seem to think about was Viola's accusing gaze, his father's unwillingness to leave the building, and the awful truth. He'd been so intent on coming home . . .

He'd forgotten that he didn't have a home to go to at all. All it was anymore was an empty house with far too many memories inside.

"Aaron, it's finally happened," Lovina blurted the minute she walked into their cozy *dawdi haus*.

Her husband, who'd been in their small kitchen pouring himself a glass of milk, paused. "*What* happened?"

She steeled her shoulders and pretended that she wasn't devastated. "Peter found out that I used to be English."

"My goodness." Carefully, he set down the glass and the carton of milk. "I suppose we should have known this day would come. You had better tell me what happened."

Her mouth suddenly dry, Lovina swallowed hard. Her insides felt twisted, like she was holding pain at bay. After forty years, it seemed that their secret was about to completely disrupt the peaceful life they'd worked so hard to build.

She opened her mouth to tell him the story, then closed it just as quickly as she searched for the right way to tell him what had gone so wrong.

"Lovina, I know it ain't easy, but it can't be helped. How did Peter find out? What did you say or do?"

She looked away, hating the accusation

in her husband's voice, but having no defense against it. Aaron was right; all of this was her fault.

When they'd married, Aaron had wanted to burn most of her mementoes from the past. She'd hated the idea and they'd argued. Leaving everything she knew had been hard enough—disposing of her whole former way of life had seemed too much to handle.

So instead, she'd hidden a few of her things in the attic. She hadn't looked inside for at least twenty years. Lately, she'd even forgotten that it was up there.

But she'd never told Aaron that she hadn't followed his directive and burned the old photos. For all this time, he'd thought she'd been obedient.

"Peter and Elsie and I were up in the attic, cleaning out some things," she began. "Uh . . . Peter found a trunk I thought was long gone. And next thing I knew, he was unwrapping my high school graduation picture."

He frowned. "I don't understand why that was even in the house. I told you to get rid of everything from your past."

She noticed he only said "her" past. As

if he had nothing to hide. Lashing out, she said, "I couldn't burn it, Aaron. Not when it brings back so many memories."

No matter what he thought, not everything about her past was forgettable.

His lips thinned. "We promised each other we'd never speak about that time. *We promised,* Lovina."

She knew he was speaking harshly because he was afraid. She knew he didn't want to remember his life before she stepped into it, and she knew he didn't want to disappoint the children.

So with that in mind, she tried to keep her emotions in check. "I didn't tell them anything about your life in Pennsylvania, Aaron. I didn't say anything even when Peter asked."

"Well, he's going to ask questions, I'm sure of it. And he's going to tell Marie, too," he added, his voice becoming panicked. "Then, no doubt, he'll tell Jacob and Sara and Aden and the rest of the *kinner.*"

"Our 'children' are all adults, Aaron. Why, even our grandchildren are all adults. The twins are twenty-two." Remembering their other secrets, she sighed, "Aaron, maybe it's time to let them know about everything."

"Definitely not."

"But—"

"Lovina, there is no reason for that."

"There is every reason." Hesitantly, she grabbed his hands. "Maybe God wants us to start being honest with the family. Maybe that's why He had Peter open that trunk."

"Don't go bringing our Lord into this mess you've created. He didn't bring about this; you did, Lovina. For some reason, you decided to ruin our life, to threaten everything we've tried to create." He shook his head as his hands clenched. "I know something is going to become of this. Peter isn't going to let that photograph slip. He's going to ask and ask and ask until neither of us knows what to do or say about it."

"That's why I think we should simply tell the truth."

"Nee."

"What we did wasn't awful, Aaron."

He stared at her, before saying quietly, "You're right. What we did wasn't so bad. But it is all over now, and there's no way we're ever going to be able to explain it to the kids."

"They're all adults—"

"It doesn't matter how old they are, Lovina. They'll always be our kids, and children, no matter what their age, want to believe that their parents are people to be proud of."

"They might still feel that way."

He shook his head. "I doubt that."

She stood frozen as he turned and stormed out the door, into the cold, without more than his cotton shirt on. Through the window, she watched him cross the yard, bypassing the barn and keep walking. Back to the spot toward the edge of their land where they'd planted two trees. Two trees to represent his previous family.

Back in Lancaster County, he'd been married to someone else. He'd become a widower when his wife's buggy had slid off the road in a rainstorm and crashed into an oncoming truck. Looking at the calendar on the wall, she winced.

Forty-two years ago this month, he'd buried his first wife and child. Less than a year later, they'd begun dating. She'd left her old life and adopted his. And as time passed, they both agreed that no good would come from discussing his earlier marriage—it was too painful. And to prevent anyone asking questions, they decided to avoid her past as well.

So they'd compromised and had tried to pretend that neither of them had lived far different lives before their wedding day. Only in the middle of the night when she lay beside him in the dark did she think about being English, and her family, and all the things that she'd used to do. Think about the person she used to be.

And only when Aaron was terribly distraught did he take a walk to the trees he'd planted in their memory.

In forty-two years, he'd never asked her to go with him.

Worse, she'd never offered.

chapter three

Daybreak Retirement Home was four miles away from the Keims' property. Though she often walked, enjoying the time to collect her thoughts before work, and to process what had happened on her way home, in the dead of winter, she sometimes used the services of a driver to get home. The good thing about that was that she got home quickly.

The bad thing was that the short commute gave her no time to push all her work thoughts to the side. She was still thinking about Mr. Swartz and his son's sudden appearance when she walked in the back door. Eager to discuss the day's events with Elsie, she was surprised to discover that no one was around.

Viola felt an uneasy sensation on the back of her neck when she entered her home's oversize kitchen. Usually, her mother would be busily working on supper, and her grandmother would be sitting at the kitchen table, peeling potatoes or sipping hot tea. More often than not, Elsie would be there as well, her silhouette in front of the sink a calming presence.

But instead of bright, bustling, and happy chatter, all was oddly quiet.

"Hello?" she called out.

When only silence greeted her, she became more concerned. Slipping off her cloak, Viola looked around, then headed upstairs. She vaguely recalled Elsie saying that she and their father were going to help clean the attic today. Perhaps that's where they all were? It was late for such a chore, but stranger things had happened.

It was just as quiet and unnaturally still upstairs. Usually, her father would be showering after a long day in the fields, Roman would have one of his many friends over, and most of the doors would be open.

Not today.

Her parents' bedroom door was closed. As was Roman's. Viola paused by each, then kept walking to her bedroom. Suddenly, she wasn't sure she wanted to know what was going on.

Warily, she turned her door's handle. As she'd half expected, the room was dark, cool, and still.

Then she spied Elsie curled on the window seat, her plum-colored dress mixing in with the cheery flower pattern of the window seat's cushion.

"Elsie, what are you doing up here in the dark?"

Her twin spun with a look of relief. "Ah, Viola! Finally, you're home. Thank the Lord."

Viola rushed forward. As always, she worried about her sister. Elsie's failing eyesight meant she often had small accidents. Viola suspected her sister's eyesight was far worse than she let on. "What's wrong? Did something happen? Are you okay?"

Elsie waved her hand in annoyance. "I am perfectly fine. But close the door; I've got a story to tell you."

Though she usually would have grumbled about being told what to do, Viola was too curious. She turned and closed the door. Then, without even taking the time to remove her thick-soled black boots, she sat right down on the closest twin bed. "Start talking."

Elsie twisted to face her. The shade behind her edged up a bit, bringing in a little sunlight, illuminating the worry etched in her features. "So, Daed, Mommi, and I were up in the attic today."

"I know. . . ."

"It was a terrible mess up there." Elsie shook her head. "I was rather surprised about that, for sure."

Viola's impatience started to get the best of her. With effort she curled her fingers into fists and tried to stay silent. Elsie had only one way to tell a story . . . in the most roundabout way possible.

After a sigh, Elsie continued. "Well, we started going through old boxes, then next thing you know, Daed pulled out a really old trunk and Mommi got upset. She started fidgeting and saying she wanted us to stop sorting through her things."

"And?" Viola blurted.

After giving her a disapproving glare, Elsie said, "And Daed ignored her, of course. He pulled out all sorts of things that used to be our grandmother's. Then, finally, he pulled out a framed photograph."

"A picture? Of who?"

"Of Grandma." Elsie warily eyed the closed door like it was going to be thrown open any second. "It was of a woman—a girl really—in a high school cap and gown. It was a photo of Mommi at her high school graduation!"

Caught in mid-nod, Viola paused. "Wait a minute. . . . What?"

"Viola, I'm trying to tell ya that Mommi used to be English."

If Elsie had said that their not-so-agile grandmother had suddenly started doing jumping jacks in the small, cramped attic, she couldn't have been more surprised. "That doesn't make sense."

"Believe me, I know!" Looking as if she was still stunned, Elsie shook her head.

"Well, what did Mommi say?"

"Mommi got so mad at Daed when he questioned her about the photo that she looked like she might cry."

Their grandmother did not cry.

"Then, when Daed wouldn't back down, she got up and marched downstairs. She didn't even wait for Daed to help her with the steep steps."

Viola was floored. Like everyone else in the family, she'd held her grandmother up as the ultimate example of a godly Amish woman. Everything about her grandmother was perfect. Except for her terrible habit of constantly putting the rest of them down, that is.

"Poor Daed."

"I know," Elsie whispered, eyeing the door yet again. "He looked so confused. Irritated, too."

"No telling what the rest of the family is going to say."

"Do you really think he'd tell everyone?"

"Are you kidding? I would!" She wouldn't waste a minute, either. Their grandmother had reigned her superiority over them for their entire lives. "What did Mamm say?"

"I don't think she's home yet. She left this morning to go shopping with Aunt Lorene in Berlin." Elsie hopped off her perch and joined Viola on the bed, sitting so close that the skirts of their bright dresses mixed together, Elsie's plum dress complementing Viola's dark purple one.

Grabbing Viola's hand, Elsie whispered, "This changes everything, V."

"Indeed, it does." Unbidden, Viola thought about her own attitude with Ed Swartz. To her shame, she realized she'd been displaying more than a little bit of her grandmother's holier-than-thou tendencies.

Flopping backward down on the bed, she grimaced. She hated saying she was sorry, but worse than that, she hated feeling like she owed someone an apology. Well, she'd just have to find a way to tell Ed she was sorry the next time they saw each other.

But now wasn't the time to think about Ed. She couldn't imagine what dinner would be like tonight. Who knew when the tension from this would blow over. . . .

Then she remembered.

With a groan, she sat straight up again. "Oh, Elsie, we're hosting church next Sunday!"

"I know." Smiling a little, she said, "The next two weeks are going to be terrible."

"Then why are you smiling?"

"Because ever since I can remember, everyone's treated me like I was the sole imperfect Keim. The damaged one."

"That's not true. You're not damaged."

One of Elsie's brows lifted. "True or not, damaged was how I felt. But now . . . it seems that I'm not the only one with a flaw. I just might be the only one who is used to admitting it."

Yes, they did all indeed have flaws, Viola realized. Some that were far worse than a vision problem.

Some much, much worse.

The key slid into the lock easily. But the brass doorknob stuck when he turned it to the right. As always. Remembering to push the knob in slightly, he jiggled it a little harder. Finally, the lock gave way. The hinges squeaked in protest when he opened the door. As a wave of musty air sprang out to greet him, Ed peeked inside.

He was home again.

His feet felt glued to the faded and frayed welcome mat. Who would have thought it would be so hard to go inside?

Glad no one was around to see him hesitate, Ed took a deep breath, clipped the screen door open, then stepped forward. The entryway looked as dark and felt as eerily cold as a cave.

But of course it would be. No one had lived there in almost two years.

Before he knew it, he had stopped on the edge of the area rug, ready to pull off his heavy boots. Just as his mother had always insisted upon.

But his boots weren't muddy, it wouldn't make much of a difference in the dusty spaces, and, of course . . . his mother was long gone. She wouldn't be there to make sure he obeyed her dozen or so "household commandments." Funny how she'd ruled the three of them with an iron will, hidden carefully inside warm hugs, beaming smiles, and a laugh that could light up a room.

A lump formed in his throat, as the pain of his loss hit him all over again. It had been three years now, but here, standing inside the house, looking around at the entryway, the room she used to take such special care of, the pain was so intense he had trouble breathing.

The fact was, it felt like he'd lost more than just a mother. He'd lost a connection with his past that he hadn't even realized was important until it was too late.

"You need to shake this off, Edward," he

said, in a true imitation of his mother. "Nothing will get done by standing frozen in one spot."

Almost chuckling, he walked into the front room and pulled up the shades, letting light stream into the room. Next, ignoring the sheets covering the furniture, he forced himself to walk through the rest of the two-bedroom, one-bathroom house and continue to pull up shades. He even cracked open two windows, preferring the cold, fresh air to the stale scent surrounding him.

In preparation for his arrival, he'd called the gas and water company the week before. He lifted the faucet handle and saw that he did, indeed, have running water.

Another check showed that the refrigerator was cooling.

Satisfied that the necessities were taken care of, he pulled off his coat, rolled up his sleeves, and went in search of cleaning supplies. His mother had been a big fan of Pine-Sol, and he knew the fresh, piney scent would go far in restoring the old house.

After a few glitches, he'd found the mop, a bucket, and half a bottle of the cleaning liquid.

It felt good to do something with his hands. This, he could concentrate on. It would be far easier to get rid of dust and grime instead of the pain of his loss.

Ignoring the cold, he rolled up his sleeves and got to work. In no time at all, he was sponging off baseboards, window-sills, and counters. He'd just begun to mop the white linoleum floor when he heard a clatter, followed by a yip, and another clatter at the front screen door.

Dropping the mop, he quickly rushed to see what was going on, only to be greeted by a red miniature dachshund. Its tail was wagging fast enough to beat the band, right in sync with the most annoying barking he'd ever heard in his life.

"Hey, you," he said, daring to approach the tiny intruder. "What in the world are you doing here?"

Soft brown eyes met his. The little dog crept two steps closer, then lifted its head, obviously ready to be petted. He obliged and scratched the dog behind its ears. "Where's your collar?"

The dog looked well fed, but a little scraggly. No collar was to be found. When he petted its side, he realized it was chilled. No

small wonder, it was near on twenty degrees, with a chance of snow in the fore-
cast.

The dog stepped closer, then to his
amazement, snuggled closer, whether because she enjoyed the companionship or
the heat, he didn't know. "You're cold,
aren't you?"

And thirsty, too, he had no doubt.

After fetching it a little bowl of water, Ed
left the dog in the kitchen and went outside to look for its owner. But he saw no
one wandering around at all. In fact, things
looked fairly empty on the street. "Well,
this is a fine situation. I've got an old house
and a wayward dog and no clue about
what I should do with either of them."

The folks at the mission in Nicaragua
would take great pleasure in his confusion, he knew. The whole time he'd been
there, he'd taken pride in being the go-to
guy, the man who could solve any problem, no matter how big or how small.

Now, he seemed to be as frozen as the
air stinging his cheeks. He had no idea
what to do next.

A new steady stream of barking interrupted his reverie. When he went back to the dog, it stilled, eyeing him hopefully.

"You were waiting for me, weren't you?" he mused. Walking to one of the closets that lined the hall, he pulled out an old blanket from the bottom of a stack. It wasn't too dusty, so he made a little nest on the floor for the dog.

The homeless pup sniffed the blanket, looked up at him warily, then crawled right into the middle of it. Almost instantly, it slept. Just like it wasn't planning to go anywhere.

For some reason, that made Edward feel pleased. It was nice to no longer be alone.

chapter four

The next morning, when Ed returned to Daybreak, he became entangled in a rousing discussion about pie, of all things.

"Hiya, Edward," his father greeted with a distracted wave. "Pull up a chair and help me talk some sense into Mr. Showalter and this girl."

While Jacob Showalter merely laughed, Viola raised her hands to her hips. "Mr. Swartz, I don't believe that I need to be 'talked to.'"

Ed hid a smile, kind of liking that she was giving his father a run for his money. There weren't too many folks who would venture into a war of words with his formidable father. "I'll pull up a chair," Ed said, "but I don't intend to get in the middle of any argument. Especially not an argument about something as important as pie."

As Viola visibly tried to hide her smile, Ed let his lips start to curve upward. It was a pleasure to see his father looking so animated and lively. Especially when just three years ago, Ed had wondered if he'd ever see him smile brightly again.

"You'd best change your mind about that," Mr. Showalter reported from his usual spot on the overstuffed couch. "Your father here has a bee in his bonnet and won't be sidetracked."

Now he didn't even try to temper his grin. "You have a bee in your bonnet, Father?"

His *daed* brushed off his quip. "All I've been saying is that Bonnets has the best chocolate cream pie in town."

"And all I'm saying is that you're wrong, Atle. The Berlin Bakery is the best, for sure. Bonnets don't hold a candle to the Berlin's chocolate cream." Turning to Ed, Mr. Showalter raised a brow. "What do you think, Edward?"

"I have no opinion. Both bakeries sound *wunderbaar,* for sure."

But that was obviously the wrong answer. Both men's eyes flashed with annoyance. "Take a stand, man," his father chided. "Everyone has an opinion worth defending."

Defending? Ed looked at Viola. "How long has this conversation been going on?"

"Too long," she said with an amused grimace. "And there's no end in sight, either. Neither man will back down."

"Ain't no reason to," Mr. Showalter said. "My opinion is right; your father's is wrong. That's all there is to it."

"I'm sure the desserts from both restaurants are mighty good, Daed."

"Anything would taste good to you, son. As you just said, you've been at the ends of the earth, eating rice and rations."

Well, he hadn't just said that. Not exactly. Though his father did have a point. He had been far away from Amish pie bakeries.

Of course, the people at the mission in Nicaragua would also be somewhat horrified to see so much energy expended over something so insignificant. If everyone had food in his belly, well, that was a blessing in itself.

But perhaps that was the point about retiring—it gave folks an opportunity to fuss about things that didn't matter all that much.

As the conversation continued with more men and women coming out of the wood-work to voice an opinion, he became aware of two things: One, his father was not in any hurry to hear about the house and the cleaning he'd done.

And two? Viola Keim was more than a little quiet around him.

And once again, he couldn't seem to take his eyes off her.

"What do you think of that idea, Edward?"

"I'm sorry? I wasn't paying attention."

As he'd known he would, his father scowled. "What is it with you young people? I'm continually having to repeat and explain myself to you."

"Sorry—"

"I was saying, Edward, that I think we should send Viola out to get pie samples and bring them back."

Before he had time to venture an opinion, Viola shook her head. "I don't think that's a *gut* idea at all."

"Why not?"

"I canna carry all the pies back here, for one."

"And?"

"And . . . I can't afford to be buying you pies, either, Mr. Swartz."

As Ed could have predicted, that started a flurry of emptying pockets among the residents. Before long, thirty dollars in singles, fives, quarters, and dimes had been accumulated.

His father looked at the pile with pleasure. "That should be more than enough to buy two pies, Viola. Off you go now, and don't worry. Edward here will help you carry them."

She visibly blanched. "Him?"

He felt her pain. "Me?"

"Yes, and yes." Turning to his son, his *daed*'s voice turned a little snippy. "Edward, surely you don't intend to make poor Viola carry the baked goods all by herself, do you? And such a long way, too. I raised you better than that, surely."

"You raised me well, Father. But that doesn't mean this scheme is a good one."

Getting to her feet, Viola looked like she was doing everything she could to ignore his very being. "Mr. Swartz, please don't worry about me needing help. I'm certain your son isn't used to offering his services freely. I can go get your pies on my own."

Ed grunted as he felt yet another jab taken at his character. "I'm surprised you can lift your head, you're so sanctimonious, Viola."

"I'm only speaking the truth, Edward."

"The name is Ed."

"*Nee,* it's Edward," his father groused. "Your mother and I gave you a perfectly *gut* name. You should use it in its entirety, not just the first two letters."

Now it seemed he could do no right with anyone. "I should have stayed home with the wiener dog," he muttered.

"Wiener dog?" Viola asked.

"Yes. Um, somehow I've adopted a dog. A little red dachshund, somewhat down on her luck, wandered to the *haus* yesterday. I couldn't find her owner, so I made her a bed in the kitchen."

He'd even privately named her Gretta, though he wasn't in the mood to share that bit of information.

"What is going to happen to her when you leave?"

"I don't know."

Viola frowned. "If you've taken in a dog without thinking ahead to her care, that's hardly fair to the dog."

"I only just found it."

"You could have taken her to the shelter."

"Enough already, Viola. There's no need for you to be badgering me about this."

"I wasn't badgering," she countered, her cheeks staining red. "I mean, I didn't mean to badger. I was only giving my opinion."

"Which you seem to do all the time, even though we hardly know each other."

Her eyes flashed. "I'm beginning to think I know enough."

"Enough, you two," his *daed* interrupted. Just as if they were twelve years old. "Go on now, and don't tarry."

"Yes, Mr. Swartz." Viola gathered up the bills and change and put it in an envelope. "You know, I must say that you're getting terribly bossy."

His father looked pleased. "I've earned the right to be bossy. I'm an old man."

"You're not that old. And once more, I must tell you that bringing you pies isn't in my job description."

"You bring me coffee. Pies aren't that different."

Viola looked about ready to pop a gasket . . . then looked at him again and chuckled. "You certainly know how to get me on my high horse, Mr. Swartz. Fine. I'll go get your pies. I'll be back when I can."

Looking extremely satisfied, his father grinned. "*Gut.* Now be a sweet girl and let my son accompany you."

"It's really not necessary." She would barely glance at him. "I'll be fine . . ."

Ed stood up as well, took the envelope full of bills and change, and slipped it into his jacket's front pocket. It sat heavy there, making his coat jingle when he stepped away from the table. "Of course I'm going to help you. I'm not going to let you go run my father's errands on your own."

"It's no trouble."

After a quick look backward at his father, who was now playing spades with Mr. Showalter, he strode to her side. "Let me go with you. Just so they won't start up another argument."

"Well, all right."

He was glad about that, though he wasn't

exactly sure why he was so relieved. She didn't like him. At all. Even so, when they left the main room and started down the tiled hallway, he stayed at her side. "You know, I am sorry for all these shenanigans. He wasn't like this when I was growing up."

To his surprise, now that they were out of his father's sight, Viola didn't look all that disgruntled. Instead, she looked amused. "I think the other residents look to him to stir things up."

Ed was slightly horrified. Suddenly, it felt as if he were the adult and his father were the child. "He seems to be doing a good job of that. I guess my *daed* can be a handful."

"He's a kind man." She flashed a smile. "Though he keeps things lively, I'd rather it be that way instead of boring. And he's never mean or short-tempered."

"I bet." He glanced her way again. "I hope you realize he's a master manipulator. He wasn't near as chatty when I was growing up, but he never was shy about getting me to do things his way."

"I've gotten that impression." She stopped

at the door. "Truly, if you'd rather stay here, that is all right with me. I don't need your help."

Her voice told him that she didn't want to accept it, either. Which, of course, made him want to help her all the more. "Are you always this independent?"

Her eyes widened, looking like she was taken aback—then she nodded. "Maybe I am."

"You're not sure?"

Now her cheeks turned a becoming rosy shade. "All right. Probably. But most don't have a problem with it." Lifting her chin a bit, she said, "Most folks enjoy having someone take charge."

"Lucky for you!"

After a quick stop in the coat room to put on her coat and mittens, as well as her black bonnet, she stopped at the office and spoke to Mrs. Ames.

After she signed out, they exited the building side by side and headed down Main Street. It was nice that the retirement home was so close to town. This part of Berlin was filled with shops and older homes and lovely wide sidewalks. Not too

many other people were out, just a few
tourists and a jogger or two. The day was
chilly, and his body, now more used to the
tropical temperatures, chilled instantly.

But besides the cold, he had to admit to
enjoying the beauty of the winter day. The
trees' branches that surrounded them
were bare, and the ground still had patches
of snow in shady sections of grass. A few
houses that they passed still had their pine
wreathes hanging on their doors. The fra-
grant bursts of green brightened the walk.

But not as much as Viola did.

Actually, it took everything he had to not
continually stare at her. The problem with
Viola Keim was that she was flat-out beautiful. She was slim and graceful, and had
dark hair that looked like it would feel like
satin against his hands. Matching brown
eyes seemed to say too much and nothing, all at the same time.

She was so completely different from
the women he'd been around for the last
two years. He'd either been around the Nic-
araguan women who were so delicate,
he felt as if a strong wind would blow them
away. And the Amish women working in

the mission were mostly older women, no one who would make him look twice.

But more important, none of them seemed to be comfortable around him. Whether it was because he was a man and they were women—or because it was in their nature to be circumspect around men of marriageable age, he didn't know.

He wasn't used to it. Growing up, he'd never had a problem flirting with girls in his church district. He'd been blessed with a great many friends of both sexes, which had given him a confidence that he'd sometimes had to keep in check.

But now that he was around Viola? She didn't avoid him like the women in Nicaragua. She simply didn't like him.

Which, for some perverse reason, appealed to him all the more.

He glanced her way again. Viola, why even her name was ladylike. It was no wonder his father had been smitten with her!

When she entered the room, it was as if a new force had just blown in. Today she wore a bright pink dress, which made her cheeks look rose-colored. And her voice was so melodic, he found himself baiting her, just so she would talk a little bit more. To his amusement, he seemed to be following in his father's footsteps . . . he was smitten—and he hardly knew her.

"So, does my *daed* send you on these fool's errands often?"

She turned to him sharply, then thawed when she saw his almost innocent expression. "*Nee.* He's been known to have me fetch him blankets or tea or coffee or cards or books . . . but this is the first chocolate-pie mission."

"Is he so needy?"

"He's a character, that's what he is. I truly don't mind. He has no one else, you know."

Ah. Yet another jab. "He and I made the decision for him to go to the home together, Viola." Not that it was any of her business.

She visibly winced. "I didn't mean to sound as harsh as I did. I'm beginning to see that he's happy, living at the retirement home."

"He is. Though I'm a bit surprised by how happy. I thought he'd be content at Daybreak, but that he'd also jump at the chance to go back home for a while."

"And he didn't jump, did he?"

"Nope. But I suppose I can't blame him.

Our house is no longer the happy place it once was," he said before he could take back the words. Well, he might as well explain. "Ever since my mother died, it only holds sad memories."

Her dark brown eyes clouded with sympathy. "Yes, I can imagine that."

A new sense of peace drifted between them. Almost tangibly, he could feel some of her anger toward him dissipate.

She smiled, the first real smile she'd directed his way. "Going back to this fool's errand, I have to say that I have a feeling if we do a good job, it won't be the last." She smiled and a dimple appeared. "He's a terrible jokester. Was he always like that?"

"Not so much. My mother kept a fairly tight rein on him. She didn't have any patience for a lot of teasing. But he definitely tried to get her dander up."

"There was only the three of you?"

He nodded. "I was their surprise baby, more than they expected, I guess." What he didn't dare confide were all of his parents' comments about how special he was. They'd told him time and again that he must have been born to them for a reason. That God had a plan for him, to be born when his parents had long since given up having a family full of *kinner.*

"And what about your other relatives?" she asked. "What do they think of your mission work, and of your *daed* living in the retirement home?"

He was beginning to feel interrogated again. "I have none living in the area. My parents were youngest children, and they moved out to Berlin on their own. I'm getting the sense that your home wasn't like that?"

"Oh, no. I still live with my brother and twin sister, and parents. And grandparents. And we have aunts and uncles and cousins nearby, too. Family is everything with my family." She smiled for an instant, then, before his eyes, looked crestfallen, too.

There was something in her tone that sent off warning signals inside him. But he couldn't quite figure out what she said that was wrong.

"You're blessed to be surrounded by so much love and support."

"Jah."

"I guess you've never had to worry about being alone."

Still looking perturbed, she shook her

head. "No . . . No, I haven't. I grew up thinking my family was the best."

"I imagine everyone thinks that about their family. I grew up thinking that, too, even though there was only the three of us."

"Even if I no longer feel that my family is perfect, I have chosen to stay near them."

"Most women do."

"As do most men. At least most Amish men."

"Just because I decided to enter into the mission field, it doesn't mean we are all that different. "

"Then perhaps it's only our feelings about family that are different."

"I love my father, Viola."

"I'm sure you do. But the fact of the matter is that your dear father is in an old folks' home, Ed. You put him there while you went off to live in a foreign country."

He held his temper in check with effort— but only barely. "You're making it sound like all I do in Nicaragua is hang out and go swimming."

"Oh, I know you do all kinds of good works. Each letter is filled with all your good, charitable efforts. I'm surprised you can sleep at night, your works are so special."

"Please, don't hold back. Tell me what you really think," he said as he held the door for her to the Berlin Bakery.

Before she could deliver any more biting commentary on his life, he marched up to the counter. "I need one chocolate cream pie, Marcia. And could you box it up carefully?"

Marcia smiled brightly. "Of course, Edward. It is so *gut* to see you! You should stop by the *haus* and tell us all about your time in South America. We're so proud of you."

Though it wasn't nice, he sent a smug look Viola's way.

She glared back. Unimpressed.

Stung, he ignored her for a few more moments, preferring to visit with Marcia about her parents and sisters. After he paid, and retrieved the pie, he turned back to his surly companion. "Are you ready to continue our errands?"

"Yes. Of course," she said after a moment's pause. "But I'm going to carry the pie."

"Fine. You can carry them both for all I care."

chapter five

The knocking came again, this time a little bit louder, and with a little more force.

"Peter, are you all right?" Marie asked from outside the bathroom door. "You've been in there for quite some time."

Sitting on the bathroom floor, the cold from the ceramic tiles seeping through the thin fabric of his wool pants, Peter was tempted to smile. Because if he knew anything, it was that he was mighty far from being "all right."

At the moment he was reduced to hiding in his own bathroom, afraid to answer his wife's calls. He'd never dreamed he would sink so low.

During breakfast, the familiar anger and frustration had coursed through him, as both of his parents steadfastly refused to discuss the photograph.

Even when he'd pressed the issue.

"It's not right, this game you're playing with us," he'd said to them. "All of us deserve to know about your past."

His father had stared back at him in the cool way he seemed to have perfected over the last sixty years. "I disagree."

Years ago, his father's implacable gaze would have rendered him silent.

Now he wasn't ready to give up so easily. Turning to his mother, he'd said, " I know Sam and Lorene would feel as I do, Mamm. Your children need to know the truth about how you grew up and how you joined our faith."

"I don't see why my reasons would have any effect on you. The past is long gone, Peter. Nothing I tell you will change that."

She was right. But years of lying to them about her childhood was hard to swallow. All they'd ever known was that their parents had moved to Ohio soon after they married because the land was far cheaper than in Lancaster County. His *mamm* never mentioned her parents, and his father had only mentioned his brothers in passing, saying that the distance was hard.

Peter remembered Jacob once asking about their family tree for a school project, and being promptly silenced. His mother had said that the only family that mattered was right here in Berlin.

They'd never understood their parents' silence about their extended family, but they'd quickly learned never to ask further questions.

His mother straightened, her spine as stiff as if it had been nailed to a ruler. "We will not discuss this a moment longer. I refuse to do it." She had the gall to look toward Marie. "I'd like some more *kaffi*," she said quietly. "And, Elsie, I want you to bring your grandfather some more biscuits."

Both women had done as she bid. As they'd always done.

But now it felt wrong. Seeing his sweet wife waiting on his mother, seeing Elsie look miserable—he'd felt as helpless as a child. Which, of course, was how his parents were treating him.

"We will discuss this again," he'd said.

"That is enough, Peter," his father cautioned, his voice as unwavering as a rod of steel. "You are looking for problems that don't exist. You'll cause a lifetime of regret, son."

Peter had been so stunned by his parents deftly turning the blame for their secrets into his fault for wanting to know the whole story that he'd felt physically ill.

He could only assume they were hiding something dark and terrible. It wasn't all that uncommon for *Englischers* to fall for Amish people and change their ways, joining the church after consideration and lots of study. There was nothing shameful about it. If his parents were just concealing a complicated love story, they would have told them their story long ago.

Fearing that he would lose his breakfast in front of the family, he'd practically run to the bathroom.

He cooled his face with a damp washcloth. Brushed his teeth. Took deep breaths. But the tight knot of anger steadfastly stayed put.

Finally, he gave in to temptation, pulled

out the bottle of vodka he'd taken care to hide in the back corner of the cupboard under his sink, and poured a small amount of liquor into a Dixie cup. Swallowed the alcohol in one long sip. And then poured another shot.

Almost immediately, he felt the tension in his muscles dissipate as his nerves began to steady.

And he was almost ready to go back out and confront his demons. But not quite yet. And definitely not in his wife's presence.

There was still one person who he felt always saw the best in him, and that was Marie. No way did he want to disappoint her.

"Peter?" she called again, this time accompanied with a fierce knock. "Please answer. I'm startin' to get concerned."

"I'm fine, Marie."

"Are you sure?" The doorknob jiggled. "Unlock the door."

"Not yet," he replied after vigorously washing out his mouth again with Listerine. There was no way he could come out of the room with the scent of liquor on his breath. "Marie, go on now. I'll be out in a minute."

"Are you sure?" She lowered her voice. "Do you need some help? Unlock the door, Peter, so I can come in . . ."

Glancing at himself in the mirror, he grimaced. Looking back at him was a person who was on the verge of a breakdown.

Hating who he was becoming, he gripped the countertop, and waited for his eyes to focus. "Marie, let a man have his privacy, why don'tcha? Please, don't worry so."

"I'm sorry. I didn't mean to intrude." Her words were muffled. Full of hurt. Maybe even slightly embarrassed. But he heard something else, too. A thread of worry and doubt. Yes, her tone was laced with mistrust.

Gathering the last vestiges of his patience, he murmured, "You're not intruding, Marie. I just need one more moment alone. I'll be right out. I promise."

He heard shuffling on the other side. "If you're sure . . ."

"I am very sure."

When he heard her walk away, he hid the bottle back under the sink, behind an old assortment of shampoo and bars of soap and tissue.

After twenty-five years of marriage, his wife was starting to mistrust him.

He had married a smart woman.

And he was starting to feel as if she'd married a very weak man.

Something was going to need to be done soon. He couldn't continue the way he was, holding everything inside, pretending he was fine when he wasn't. All the subterfuge was taking a toll on his body and his soul. He had the sweetest wife in the world. And she put up with so much. She surely didn't deserve the man that he'd become.

Schooling his features, he opened the door and walked out. To his surprise, she hadn't gone far. She was standing at the end of the hall, eyeing him warily.

With a smile, he said, "There. I'm out now. What was so important that it couldn't wait? Did you need something?"

She stepped backward, obviously disturbed by his tone. "As a matter of fact, yes. But now I'm wondering if, perhaps, you need to tell me something instead." Her gaze seemed to take in every inch of him. And it was obvious that she saw something that didn't please her.

"I don't need to tell you a thing."

Her eyebrows rose. "You sound like your mother."

The glint in her eyes told him she was teasing. "I hope I don't. She's the last person I want to emulate right now."

"Then Peter—"

Folding his arms over his chest, he fought to act like nothing in the world could ever be wrong. "Don't fuss. I am fine, Marie."

"Are you sure? Because, Peter, if you have a problem, I could help you. That's what husbands and wives do for each other."

"Of course they do. And you know I would move heaven and earth to give you help, if that's what you needed."

"I feel the same way."

"I'm glad of that." He gently rubbed his calloused thumb along the fine line of her cheekbone before turning and starting down the stairs. He wasn't sure about anything anymore. Not about his drinking, not about his family. But he couldn't tell her that.

She followed at his heels.

As he plodded down the steep staircase, trying to maintain his balance, he shot off a question. "Was there something you wanted to talk about now that we've determined that I am fine?"

"*Jah.* It's about your mother."

He swayed a bit and blamed it on the topic. He loved his parents. But were they also a source of hurt and stress in his life? Always!

As they came to the landing, Marie rushed to his side. "Peter, you almost stumbled. This is not like you. Are you all right?"

Though he knew it hurt her feelings, he shrugged off her touch. "I am perfectly fine, Marie." When they reached the kitchen, he said, "Now, tell me. What's wrong with Mamm now?"

"I think she's having a mighty difficult time with the photo being discovered."

"I imagine she is."

She lowered her voice. "And even more, I fear that your father is upset with her. When you left, Aaron didn't eat the biscuit Elsie brought him. Instead, he got up from the table in an all-fire hurry and left Lovina sitting alone."

"Well, then, she can join our sorry club of disappointed folks. I'm having a difficult time accepting the fact that she's been hiding something so important from us all."

"What do you think we should do?"

Her question took him off guard. Never had he ever felt that he should "do" anything about his parents. They were in charge. He adapted. That was the way of things and always had been. "You heard me try to coax them into talking. Until they change their minds, I don't think we can do a thing."

"Nothing?" His wife looked aghast. "But this news of hers . . ."

"What can be done? Marie, they've always been secretive. Don't you remember that supper when Elsie asked my parents how they met? She couldn't have been more than seven, but they both scolded her for asking about things that were none of her business. That photograph only confirms that they had every reason to be secretive. We should have suspected something long ago."

"I think this is a sign that we need to have a real discussion about the relationships in this family. Perhaps we need to ask Sam and Lorene to come over."

Sam and Lorene were the only other

siblings who'd stayed in the area. The others had moved far enough away to begin new lives. More than once, Peter had found himself envying their distance and independence, especially his brother Jacob who lived all the way out in Shipshewana, Indiana. It had taken a lot of strength for the eldest son to not do what was expected and move into the main house when he married.

But Jacob had never been shy about his desire to live away from his parents.

Peter had always taken the role of the peacemaker in the family. Now he was wondering if perhaps he'd just been too weak to follow his own dreams. Ignoring the lump in his throat, he did his best to concentrate on the topic at hand. "Sam would come over, but I doubt Lorene would."

"Lorene would come if you asked her," Marie countered.

Peter sighed. Everything inside him wanted to back away and continue to pretend that everything was fine. But he didn't know how to do that. "I'll call Sam now. Your idea is a good one, Marie." And he knew it was, even though his stomach was tied up in knots.

"And Lorene?"

"Of course, I will go visit with Lorene and ask her to join us." Anxious to get away from her piercing gaze, he turned and walked to the cloak room. With methodical motions, he put on his wool muffler and his wool coat. His hat and gloves. "I'll be back in a few hours, Marie."

"Are you sure you're feeling well enough to drive the buggy? The roads will be busy."

"Why wouldn't I be all right?"

Her anxious gaze turned steady. "Because we both know your mother isn't the only one hiding things."

She walked away before he had a chance to reply. Which was a very good thing, of course.

Because he had no earthly idea what he was going to tell her. No woman wanted to hear that her husband had a drinking problem, and that it had been going on for more than a year.

Especially not an Amish woman.

And especially not Marie.

It didn't take long to get to Lorene's place of work by buggy. His thirty-two-year-old sister was still unmarried, and a few years ago, she seemed to have had more than enough of living at home. She'd announced one day that she had found herself a duplex on East Miller, just a few houses down from Sam and Mary Beth, and taken a job at Himler's Cheese Shop. Located in the center of Berlin, it was within walking distance to her new home.

Their parents had been sure that Lorene's bout with independence was going to last no longer than a week. Perhaps a month at the longest. But it had been more than three years now, and if anything, Lorene seemed far more willing to speak her mind than ever before.

She was honest to a fault. But there was still a wistfulness about her that he'd always appreciated. Peter hoped one day that she would find the man she'd been looking for.

Lorene usually worked the cash register. She was especially good with numbers and working with the English, too. She was able to fill orders with ease for people who wanted to ship large quantities of the Amish-made cheese home.

His sister smiled broadly at him when he approached the front desk. "Hello, Peter. I have to say, seeing you is certainly a surprise!"

"It shouldn't be that much of a shock."

"Of course not." Looking him over, she said, "I'm glad to see you, but if you had needed something from the store, you should have told me. I would've picked something up for you and saved you the trip."

"I didn't come for food, I came to see if you could stop by the *haus* this evening."

"And you didn't care to simply call the store from the phone shanty?"

"No. It's pretty important, Lorene."

A line formed between her brows. "Now you've got me curious. See, I'd already planned to stop by. I'm going to make macaroni salad with the girls. Did no one tell you?"

"It must have slipped Marie's mind." Frankly, he was surprised any of them could concentrate on their regular schedules given what was going on. He glanced behind him to make sure he wasn't holding up a line. Since no one was waiting, he was tempted to spill everything to Lorene then and there. But it wasn't the time. "Okay, then, I'll see you tonight."

She studied him for a bit before clearing her throat. "Hold on a sec. I think we'd better talk right now. It's clear something important is going on."

Peter watched her speak to Frank, an Amish man who was one of the managers of the store. Frank looked over at Peter and waved. "Peter, hello! Cold enough for ya?"

"Hiya, Frank. It's cold enough for January, to be sure."

"Came to steal Lorene for a bit, have you?"

He hadn't, but he was fine with following Lorene's lead. "Just for a few moments. We won't be long."

Seconds later, Lorene led the way to the small eatery on the side of the store. It was set up much like a snack bar, offering pretzels, hot dogs, and an assortment of drinks and desserts. "This wasn't necessary, Lorene."

"Maybe not. In any case, I've got a break coming. Let's grab something to drink."

Because he was glad to be speaking with her anyway, he complied. After they both got cups of coffee, they sat across from each other in one of the booths. "Now, you have to tell me. What in the world is so important that you'd drive over here simply to ask me to come to the *haus* tonight? What is going on?"

There was no easy way to share the news. "It turns out Mamm was raised English."

"What?"

"We uncovered a high school graduation photo of her yesterday. When Elsie and I asked questions, she admitted that it was her."

Lorene looked as stunned as he'd felt. While he continued to fill her in, she grew more and more disturbed. She clasped her hands together so tightly that her knuckles turned white. "Peter, I have to say, I'm shocked. And, I kind of feel like crying. For most of my life, she's made me feel less than perfect. That I was letting down the long lineage of Amish *fraus*. And all while she's been keeping something like this from us?"

She shook her head in wonder. "So, what happened? How did she and Daed meet?"

"I don't know."

"Well, how old was she when she became Amish? What about Daed? Was he an *Englischer,* too? And what about her parents? She never spoke of them. Did they disown her?" Her eyes widened. "Or maybe she disowned them, just like she always used to threaten with us!"

"I don't know those answers, either." Now that she brought up all the questions, he ached for the answers, too. "You know how she is. The moment she got upset, she left. She didn't join us for supper last night. Then, when I tried to get more information from her at breakfast she turned icy."

"What did Daed do?"

"He says it's none of our business as well. Which makes me wonder if there's far more to the story. If they weren't trying to hide something else, they would've been far more open."

Lorene pursed her lips, still in shock.

"Marie and the girls are upset. Actually, Marie thought it would be best if you and Sam came over this evening to talk about things with Mamm and Daed."

"What good does she think that will do?"

Peter smiled. "I thought the same exact thing. When have our parents ever cared to hear our opinions about anything?"

"Let's see . . . Never?" Lorene quipped with more than a touch of bitterness.

"I agree with you. But, I do think Marie has a point. If we do nothing, our parents will decide that their pasts never need to be mentioned again. I don't think that is right."

"I agree." Looking into her half-full coffee cup, she sighed. "As much as I don't want to sit across from our parents and shoot questions at them, I think it needs to be done. When I think of how different our lives would have been, if we'd ever gotten even a hint that they, too, had had troubles . . . it makes me want to either scream or roll up in a ball."

"I know, Lorene." He felt terrible for her. She'd always knocked heads with their mother, and had always come out the loser in their battles.

"Have you talked to Sam yet?" she murmured. "He'll have plenty to say, too."

"I'm going to go see Samuel next."

"You don't need to. I'll tell him and Mary Beth when I get off work this afternoon. I'll stop by their *haus* on the way home."

"I hope he'll want to join us."

"He will. And we'll need to call the others." Her eyes widened. "What do you think Jacob is going to say?"

As the eldest of the six of them, Jacob had borne the brunt of their parents' criticism. He'd moved to Indiana the moment he'd met his wife. Peter could remember him coming back only a handful of times over the last twenty years. "Only God knows the answer to that, I'm afraid. But something tells me that Jacob is not going to take this well."

"He won't, and neither will Aden or Sara." After glancing to her right to make sure no one was eavesdropping, she murmured, "We're a dysfunctional lot for a reason, Peter. I only hope this news doesn't throw us all into a bigger mess than we're already in."

She was teasing, of course. But there was more than a grain of truth to what she was saying. Each one of them bore the scars of their parents' interference and constant putdowns.

She closed her eyes. "Peter, when I think of what she put me through with John Miller, I want to scream."

"John Miller?" He tried to place the man—and Lorene's relationship with him. "He's the woodworker, right?"

"He used to simply be a woodworker.

Now he owns one of the most successful businesses in Berlin, Miller's Fine Furniture. He must have fifty people working for him."

"I've seen the store, but I didn't know you had ties to the owner."

"I don't. I mean, not anymore. John and I tried to court, but Mamm made me stop seeing him because she didn't think the Millers were good enough."

"What was wrong with them?"

"John's mother passed away when he was young, and his daed never really recovered from it, I'm afraid. John and his twin brother, Thomas, were always the kids who needed a shower, who needed cleaner clothes. . . ." She shrugged. "They'd needed a lot of things, I suppose."

Frowning, Lorene added, "I knew that I wasn't any better than John, but I was too afraid of making Mamm upset with me for the rest of my life to go up against her. So I began to have doubts about him." Quietly, she added, "Finally, I pushed John away."

"I'm sorry, Lorene." Yes, it was becoming increasingly obvious that each one of them had gone to a great deal of trouble to try to keep up appearances that the Keims were one of the finest families in the area.

It would be humbling for everyone to finally discover the truth—that they were no better than anyone else.

And perhaps a great deal worse.

chapter six

After Lorene clocked out, she decided to find her boss before she hitched up her buggy and drove home. "What do you know about John Miller?" she asked Frank without preamble.

Her boss knew just about everyone in Berlin, and everyone came to him for information about people or places, or even the history of the town.

Which was why he didn't seem surprised by her inquiry and put down the box he was carrying to calmly consider her question.

"John Miller? Hmm . . . Well, he has a

mighty *gut* business. It's Miller's Fine Furniture, you know."

She'd known that, but had only recently discovered the news. There were so many families with the last name *Miller,* she'd never connected the down-on-his-luck man she once loved with the well-run business. "Is he married?"

Frank thought about it for a moment, then shook his head. "I don't think so. Don't know why, either." He shrugged. "Guess the Lord hasn't decided to bless him with romance yet. Why all the questions? Are you wantin' furniture?"

"Maybe." She looked around. "Frank, do you know if Kim is still here today?"

"I do. She's in the office."

"Danke."

Two minutes of conversation gave her the answer she needed. Kim would be happy to drive her over to the furniture store, then back to the store so she could pick up her buggy and head to Peter's. And she could leave within the next few minutes.

That was all the news Lorene needed to confirm her sudden plan. She wasn't going to waste another moment wondering about what could have happened with her and John Miller.

Fifteen minutes later, Kim had parked her sedan and was popping open a can of soda and slipping a book out of her purse. "Take all the time you want, Lorene. The only thing I've got waiting at home is laundry. I'm happy enough to sit here in the car and read."

"Thanks." She exited the car, and walked up to the store. As soon as she entered, she was charmed by the smell of lemon oil and freshly cut wood.

"May I help you?" A lovely blond-haired girl about Elsie's and Viola's age approached as Lorene gently closed the door behind her.

Here went nothing. "I'm looking for John Miller. Is he in?"

"Mr. Miller?"

"Yes. There's a personal matter I need to speak to him about."

Still looking doubtful, the girl turned around and went into a back room. "He'll be right out," she said when she returned.

"Danke."

Then, out came John Miller and her heart

seemed to race. His blond hair was shorter than she remembered, but his posture was just as straight and proud. Furthermore, his cheeks were still clean-shaven, signifying that Frank was right—he'd never married. And even from across the room, she noticed that his eyes were as mesmerizing as ever, a dark green as deep as the forest.

He strode toward her, his handsome face looking professional and calm. But then he stopped and stared. "Lorene?"

"Yes. Hi, John."

He approached her far more slowly. So slowly, she felt like he wished he were walking backward. So slowly, the girl who worked for him couldn't seem to concentrate on anything else but the two of them.

When he was about two feet in front of her, he stopped. Looked her up and down. "Katie said you had something to say of a personal nature. What could it possibly be?"

His tone was cool. His expression was mistrustful. And after all this time, full of hurt.

Her mouth went dry, and she felt twice the fool. What had she expected? That he was going to see her and run into her arms?

She backed up a step. "You know what? I think I just made a big mistake. Bigger even than the one I made ten years ago. I'm so sorry, John. I mean, I'm so sorry to trouble you." Turning, she practically ran to the door.

It didn't escape her notice that John didn't try to follow. Well, what had she expected? She'd practically made it a lifelong pursuit to avoid him for the last ten years. Had she really thought he'd suddenly pursue her now that she'd shown up to talk to him?

Was she truly that full of herself?

As she slowly walked back to Kim's car, Lorene wondered if she was far more like her mother than she'd thought.

"I just don't understand why Ed is so stubborn," Viola exclaimed. "And argumentative! Every time I say something, he acts like he's getting ready to disagree."

Giving their aunt Lorene a not-too-subtle look, Elsie paused in her stirring. She and her twin were putting together a big dish of macaroni salad while across the kitchen, Aunt Lorene was chopping squash and sweet potatoes for a casserole for supper. Sam and Mary Beth and their children were coming over.

"I saw that look," Viola quipped.

"What look?" Elsie replied, not too innocently.

"You know . . ."

"It could be that we're a little busy at the moment," Lorene murmured. "The moment I got here, your mother was putting the roasters in the oven." Yes, everything in their house was in a great uproar, thanks to her grandmother's revelation. Everyone seemed to be walking on eggshells, too.

Except for Elsie. She seemed to be greatly amused by Viola's complaining. "Sounds like Ed made quite an impression on you," Elsie said.

"A bad impression."

"Perhaps," Elsie said with a secret smile.

"What is that supposed to mean?"

"Only that you seem to mention this man a lot. I mean a lot, considering that you don't care for him too much."

"I like his father. And I worry about him. Here he is spending every evening in the retirement home instead of his own house."

"Didn't you tell me Mr. Swartz didn't want to leave the retirement home while Edward was here?"

"Well, *jah*," she said grudgingly.

"And, though I haven't met Mr. Swartz, I've gotten the impression that he doesn't do much he doesn't want to do."

"He's no pushover, for sure."

Elsie added the last of the macaroni and stirred. "Then why are you upset about this?"

"I'm not upset. I am just saying that I think a son ought to do more for his parents. That's all."

"Viola, I have to agree with your sister," Aunt Lorene said, her voice laced with merriment. "You can't seem to stop talking about Edward Swartz. And so far nothing he's been doing sounds terrible. Every person has to go out and make their life. I imagine his life in the mission field hasn't been an easy one."

"Probably not. Though I don't exactly know what he was doing over there. His letters to his father talked mostly about the vegetation and weather."

"Maybe you should talk to him about that," she said as she pushed one casserole dish to the side, then began chopping up stalks of celery.

"Oh, right." She looked up as her aunt's tone finally filtered through. "You're teasing me."

"Just a little bit," Lorene said in that gentle way of hers. "And, there's nothing wrong with being smitten with a handsome man like Ed, who's had an interesting life, too. He sounds *goot gukkich.*"

Viola felt her cheeks heat by the comment. It was true, she did find Edward terribly handsome. She also liked how he was no pushover. He stood up to her easily and kept her on her toes. But she'd hoped that she could have kept her feelings a secret for a little longer.

Besides, looks only counted for so much. Hadn't her mother told her that time and again? "I am most certainly not smitten with Edward. He just happens to be on my mind," she said airily. "I'm only warning you both about him."

Elsie blinked. "Because?"

"Because he is exasperating."

Lorene and Elsie exchanged amused glances. "Because?" Elsie asked again.

"Because he's a man who isn't shy about

stating his mind. He gives opinions without the slightest bit of prompting."

Elsie's smile turned into a full-fledged grin. "Hmm. Sounds like someone else I know."

Viola knew this had to be a terrible mistake, bringing Edward's name into her house. But no matter how hard she tried, she couldn't seem to stop thinking about him! About how he was continually baiting her.

Or about how he'd stayed close to her side the whole time they were walking with those pies in their arms. Or how he'd grinned as his father had stared at the pies like they were the most amazing things on earth.

No matter how difficult she found him to be, there was no denying that he loved his father very much.

"Sorry. I'll stop talking about him."

"I hope you don't. It's fun to hear about someone new." After a look behind her, Elsie lowered her voice. "Besides, it's a *verra* nice change from what everyone else is focused on."

Only because their mother was in the barn, supervising Roman and their father unloading the church benches for next Sunday's services did Viola dare mention the elephant in the room. "Have you spoken to Mommi about being English? I've been dying to know why she's been keeping her past a secret all this time."

"She hasn't said a word to me," Elsie murmured. "But I haven't asked, either. I'm afraid to."

Lorene chuckled. "Viola, has this preoccupation of Edward ruined your mind? There's no way on earth any of us is going to badger my mother about her secret life without the others there, too."

Viola winced. Her aunt's voice was tinged with bitterness. "Do you think any of your other brothers had any idea that Grandmother was raised English?"

"I promise you, none of us had any idea. We all grew up thinking that our mother was as close to perfect as a person could get . . . and that we would never measure up."

"Perhaps some secrets should be kept secrets," Elsie said quietly.

"Not that kind of secret!" Viola said. "Aunt Lorene, is that why Uncle Samuel and Aunt Mary Beth are coming over?"

"But of course. We hope to talk to our parents this evening. No matter what the secret is, it's better for it to be out in the open."

"I want to be there, too. I think we should all go talk to Mommi and tell her that she has to tell us the whole story."

Lorene shook her head. "It's not that easy. And because of that, I certainly don't think the two of you or Roman needs to be there."

"We're not *kinner* anymore, Aunt Lorene," Elsie pointed out. "We've been affected by this as well."

Viola piggybacked on her twin's statement. "If all of this comes out in the open, some members in the community will certainly have plenty to say."

"That is true."

After another quick glance at the door, Viola said, "Have you talked to any of my aunts and uncles?"

"I talked to Sam and Mary Beth, of course." Biting her lip, she added, "By now I'm sure everyone else in the family knows. Samuel said he was going to leave messages on the rest of the family's phones."

Looking apprehensive, Viola pulled some

rolls out of the oven. "What did Uncle Sam and Aunt Mary Beth think?"

"They were as stunned as me. I'm afraid Samuel was terribly upset. I guess he was good friends with an *Englischer* during his *rumspringa*. Mamm and Daed gave him a lot of grief for hanging out with people 'not like us.'"

Elsie winced. "Ouch."

Lorene thought that comment said it all. "That's what I thought, too, dear," she said wryly. "Anyway, Sam says he's going to have a lot to say tonight."

"What about you?" Viola asked. "Are you planning to say a lot, too?"

"Nee."

"Why not?" Elsie asked.

After a long moment, she said, "It's no secret that I don't have a terribly good relationship with my *mamm.* This is just making it harder. I don't have much to say, not anymore. I think it would be best if I keep my head in the sand instead. Even though it's nothing to be proud of, for sure."

"What happened with you two?" Viola blurted. "If you don't mind me asking, that is."

As Aunt Lorene looked like she was

struggling to answer, Elsie glared at her. "What happened with Aunt Lorene is none of our business, Viola."

Only her twin could make her feel shame like this. "I'm sorry. Elsie's right. Please, forget I asked."

Her backing off seemed to help Lorene. Shrugging, she said, "Actually, now that I think about it, it's not that big of a secret. Only painful." She sighed. "The problems with Mamm go back to ten years ago. I was seeing a man I really liked. My mother didn't think he was suitable but I disagreed."

"What happened? Did you see him anyway?"

"Why was he unsuitable?" Elsie added.

Viola heaped on another question. "Was he not Amish?"

"Oh, you two. Sometimes when you twins start finishing each other's thoughts, it can be maddening!" After a moment, she said, "John was Amish, but he was . . . scruffy. And I was tempted to see him more. . . ."

Elsie pushed the dish she was filling away. "I'm not even going to pretend I'm interested in cooking right now. Tell us more."

"What do you mean, he was scruffy?" Viola asked.

Lorene frowned. "Goodness, perhaps saying he was scruffy wasn't the kindest way to describe him. He was a *gut* man, but a bit rough around the edges. He didn't have any money to speak of. His family was poor, and his mother died young. So his clothes were always a little dirty, and never quite fit right. Later, his father wasn't able to care for him and his brother."

"What happened to him?"

"An uncle took the boys in. That was good, but the uncle was something of a recluse." Her voice cracked, illustrating just how affected she still was by the bitter-sweet memories. "John Miller was someone who could have been so much more, if he'd just had someone who believed in him."

"But you believed in him, right?" Elsie prodded, her eyes wide.

"I did." Blushing a little bit, Lorene added, "He was so kind to me, and he was sensitive. I could talk to him about almost anything. I was sure he was the right man for me. But, of course, my mother didn't see things that way."

Caught up in the story, Viola blurted, "That shouldn't matter."

"It did at the time." Tilting her head down, she winced. "When I was with John, I felt like the prettiest, smartest, most special girl in the room. He believed in me, you see." She sighed. "I suppose I should have tried harder for him to be accepted. . . ."

"What did Daed say?"

"Peter? Oh, gosh, I never told your father. I never told any of my siblings. I'm the youngest, you know. And when my parents told me that I couldn't see him anymore, no matter what, well, after a few weeks of arguing, I realized that I wasn't going to win that battle. I certainly wasn't going to get the rest of the family involved!"

"Because you were afraid that they'd side with your parents, too?"

"I had thought they would." Her bottom lip trembled. "But now? I'm not so sure. Maybe I should have trusted them more?" Softly she added, "If I had trusted myself more, things might have turned out far different."

"Where is John Miller now?" Elsie asked. "Did he move away?"

"Oh, no. His brother moved away, but he's still here."

"I've never heard of him," Viola said.

"No reason why you should have. There are thousands of Amish in Holmes County. Plus, John doesn't belong to our church district."

After exchanging a look with Elsie, Viola said, "You should go talk to him, Aunt Lorene."

"Actually, I did. Today."

Viola reached out and squeezed her sister's hand. "And? Are you two still in love after all this time?"

A shadow slipped into her expression. "I'm afraid not. John owns his own furniture store now. He's quite successful. But it was clear he still hasn't forgotten how I broke things off. I fear he'll never forgive me."

"All you have to do is explain things, Lorene," Elsie said in a rush. "I'm sure once he hears that you regret things, he'll understand."

"I'm afraid it's not that easy. It's been ten years. And that's a mighty long time to wait to tell someone that you're sorry." Picking up a potato, she said, "I only told you that story . . . Gosh, now I don't even know why I told you. It's not important. Not anymore."

"Maybe he's your true love," Elsie murmured. With a glint in her eye, she added, "Just like Edward might be Viola's true love."

Lorene chuckled.

Viola didn't throw a piece of the carrot she was cutting at her sister because her aunt was there. But she was tempted to. "Edward is not my true love," she said firmly.

"Care to tell me who you are speaking of, Viola?" her mother said from the doorway.

Her mother's appearance felt like a cold wind, cooling off all thoughts of love and impossible relationships. "No. I mean, we're not talking about anything. It's nothing," she replied over her sister's snickers.

"Sure about that?"

"Yes, Mamm."

"All right then," she murmured before leaving again.

"Gotcha!" Elsie said with a laugh.

"You certainly did." One day she was going to get Elsie back. She was sure of that!

chapter seven

Lorene had always adored her brother Sam. He'd been the one who looked out for her, and had the kindest disposition. He'd tempered their eldest brother Jacob's bossy personality and he'd also been the first to marry.

Sam seemed to have been born to make others feel important and loved.

But he looked like a completely different person at the moment. His face looked as hard as stone as he sat beside his wife in the small living area of the *dawdi haus*. They'd decided to confront their parents there so they couldn't walk away from the discussion.

Her mother and father sat still as statues on two ladderback chairs in front of the fireplace. Peter and Marie sat on two other chairs. Though Roman, Elsie, and Viola had wanted to join in the discussion, Sam had asked that they look after his three kids instead. Daniel, David, and Dora were just old enough to understand that all of them were upset, but probably too young to fully understand the reasons for their pain.

Everyone looked like they sincerely wished they were somewhere else. Anyplace else.

"You needn't have arranged this inquisition, Peter," their father said. "There isn't anything to discuss."

"You know that's not true."

"I agree," Sam said. "Mamm, I was terribly surprised to hear your news. And we need to talk about it."

"It doesn't matter, Samuel. All that was years ago."

"But it does," Lorene blurted before she thought better of it. "All our lives, you acted like you never made a mistake in your life."

"Joining the Amish wasn't a mistake, daughter. It was the best thing I ever did."

"Why? What made you adopt the faith? And what about your parents? You never speak of them. What did they think?" Sam paused, then asked yet another question that had been on everyone's mind. "Are they even alive?"

"That is none of your business," their usually quiet father said.

"I disagree," Samuel countered.

Although Aaron was now at least fifty pounds lighter than his sons, he still glared at them, immediately tempering their feisty words. "You will mind your tongue."

Looking from Peter to Marie to Sam to Mary Beth, Lorene winced. Oh, but this was going badly. "Why don't you two simply tell us what happened?" she said in a reasonable tone. "Then we wouldn't be asking you so many questions."

Her parents exchanged glances.

"I don't think so," their father said. "What happened is in the past. It won't help any of you to know what we did back in Pennsylvania before you were born. Besides, it's our concern, not yours."

Lorene felt her two brothers flinch in surprise.

"Come on," Peter said, exasperated. "I'm not going to let you push this off like it was some minor incident in your youth. We're talking about a major decision that affected your whole lives."

Their father glared through the thick lenses of his silver wire-rimmed glasses. "We are still your parents, and deserve your respect, son."

The words stung, as their father had no doubt intended them to. Aaron Keim had always been a gentle man. He'd never raised a hand to them. When they were all in school, their neighbors would remark about how he could corral six children so easily with only one meaningful look.

Now, Lorene realized that she'd been following her siblings' examples. They had obeyed instantly, and so she had wanted to obey instantly, as well.

Now, here they were again. Once again bristling under their parents' stern gazes. Even after thirty years, it was difficult to argue with them.

"Our need to understand your past isn't some childish whim, Mamm," Sam said slowly. "I have *kinner* now, too. I understand a parent's need for privacy, but this is beyond that."

Glaring, their mother blurted, "It wasn't a whole other life, Samuel. It was simply a long time ago, and one I promised myself I'd soon forget."

"But you can't forget the past. Not really," Lorene murmured.

Her father blinked. For a moment Lorene was sure he was about to agree with her. But then his expression hardened, in tune with his voice. "Daughter, I'm in no hurry to hear more of your complaints, and I don't intend to answer any of your questions, either. This discussion is over."

Something snapped inside of Lorene. Pain from denying herself happiness bubbled up inside her like a pot that had been on the burner too long. "But it isn't over."

All her life, she'd backed down. But now was different. Maybe she finally felt old enough to speak her mind. Maybe she finally felt like she had nothing to lose—after all, she'd never found a man like John. She'd never found anyone who had claimed her heart like he had.

Letting her emotions guide her, she stood

up. "You can't do this. You two can't simply refuse to talk about the past."

"Don't speak to me in that tone, Lorene. Mind your manners."

There went the rest of her temper—it sailed right out the door with the last of her control. "I am not a child."

"Then stop acting like one."

"Actually, for the first time in my life, I think I'm finally acting like an adult. No longer will I simply listen to your directives and follow your rules. Not after you did everything you could to ruin my life." Then, before she took the time to weigh the consequences of her actions, she blurted out what she was really thinking, "Not after John."

While Peter remained quiet, Samuel darted a confused look her way. "Who in the world is John?" he asked.

Though she'd wanted to avoid the subject, it seemed she couldn't help herself. "John Miller is the man I was in love with ten years ago. He's the man I wanted to marry. He's the man Mamm and Daed refused to let me see, saying he wasn't good enough for me."

"He wasn't," her mother said. "Why are

you even mentioning him? Have you been seeing him again?"

"No. He doesn't want to see me," she said with as much dignity as she could muster.

Awkwardly, her mother stood up and faced her. But where before there was always a certain sweet tenderness, now panic warred with anger in the lines of her face. "Lorene, I suppose blaming me for your troubles makes you feel better. And you're right. I did warn you against him. But you didn't put up much of a fight, did you?"

She was stunned. "You expected me to fight you?"

"I expected you to fight for your future—if he really meant something to you. But you didn't. And once more, you never sought him out over the years." Her voice lowered, sounding thick with disdain. "That there is all you need to know, ain't so? You can blame me all you want, but your loneliness isn't my fault. You made that choice all on your own. You gave up easily."

"But—"

She held up a hand. "There is no 'but.' All these years have passed and you never said a word. You can pretend that you cared, but you obviously didn't. A woman in love would have fought, Lorene. A woman in love would have tried harder. I did."

Looking down her nose at Lorene, she sniffed. "That is the kind of thing you need to think about. Not what *I* did wrong . . . but what *you* have done."

As their mother turned and walked to her bedroom, Lorene stood motionless, frozen by the spiteful words. A whole decade of her life had passed in silence. She'd wasted so much time trying to do the right thing, to be the good daughter. And now she found out that her mother hadn't even respected her choices! No; instead of respecting her, she'd looked down on her with contempt.

There, in the circle of her brothers and their wives, Lorene felt angry and embarrassed. What had just happened?

One by one, Sam, Peter, Mary Beth, and Marie stood up as they watched their father silently turn and follow their mother out of the room. Then they all exited the *dawdi haus.*

Even standing outside in the cold felt better than the stifling atmosphere that had settled in that room.

Raising her face to the sky, Lorene breathed in the cool air, hoping the deep breaths would calm her churning insides.

She fought to keep her tears at bay. The last thing she wanted was to start crying in front of her brothers.

But, oh, she was so sad. What a mistake her life had become!

Marie hugged her close. "Try not to take what she said to heart, Lorene," she said softly. "Lovina has always had a spiteful tongue."

Lorene stood stiffly in her embrace. She loved her sister-in-law, but she didn't think any simple words could ease the moment.

After another hug, Marie and Mary Beth went back to the main house.

Just as she started to follow, Peter reached for her arm. "Wait a moment, *shveshtah*."

"What is it?"

"Are you going to be all right?" he asked gently.

Was she? Were any of them? "I don't know."

Sam walked to her side and slipped his hand in hers. "Don't listen to Mamm."

"I'm afraid she's right, Sam."

"To someone who never lived with our parents, our *mamm*'s words might make a lot of sense. But we were all there together," he said darkly. "I know how hard it was to go against our parents. I know how certain they were about just about everything." Lowering his voice, he added, "You were a dutiful daughter, Lorene. You did everything right. You did everything you were asked to do. As they raised all of us to do."

"Yes, I was dutiful," she repeated, feeling that she hated that word even more than she thought. "I listened. I did what I was supposed to. And what did I get for that? Even more disappointment. Now it feels like I've lost years. So much time that I'll never be able to get back."

"I know."

Though she hated how weak she sounded, she murmured, "I've spent most of my life trying to be good, which was supposed to help me sleep well at night, but it never really did."

"Doing what is expected doesn't help your heart much, does it?" Peter said, a bit of melancholy in his voice. "Not in the middle of the night when old hurts remind you of why you aren't happy."

"No matter what I do, I can't seem to win."

Peter sighed. "For what it's worth, you're not alone in that, Lorene. It's how all of us feel." He glanced Sam's way. "I moved into the house because someone had to. I did everything Mamm and Daed wanted me to because I wanted them to approve. To maybe even be proud of me. To be like them."

"We all wanted to be like them."

"And until this very moment," Sam said, "I didn't think we'd ever come close. I thought each of us was doomed to be faint copies of our parents."

Realizing that their parents were just as flawed as they were, Lorene said, "Perhaps we were all wrong. All this time, we thought we could never be good enough. But we didn't spend the last forty years lying to our children."

Peter laughed dryly. "Well, that's something I suppose."

"It certainly gives me something to think about with my three *kinner*," Sam said. "Next time one of them tells a fib, I need to remember that things could be worse!"

"Well, you know what Jacob would say," Lorene murmured.

Sam and Peter exchanged wry glances. "He'd say that things can always get worse," Sam said with a grin. "All we have to do is wait ten minutes."

Lorene chuckled. Because she and her brothers had grown up so close in age, bickering had been a constant occurrence. Their mother used to say that she would get worried when everything was running too smoothly—she'd be waiting for the other shoe to drop.

And now, here they all were, firmly embroiled in all the problems their parents had swept under the rug for years.

It seemed their mother had been right about one thing at least . . . living peacefully was only a temporary thing.

chapter eight

"Well, Gretta, I'd have to say we did our best with the lot we were given, don't you think?" Ed asked the little dog whom he'd now almost officially adopted. "If Mamm were alive, she'd tell me I did a right good job with the cleaning."

Gretta stared up at him solemnly, then turned to her new little bed. The day before he'd ended up buying a cedar-filled dog bed for her, wanting her to be comfortable when he wasn't home. She'd been pleased as punch with it—well, as soon as he'd put a small blanket on the bed so she could burrow underneath it.

The hours had been long in the house, so he'd used the time as best he could. He'd scrubbed and polished and aired out mattresses and blankets and quilts. Luckily, the weather had cooperated and he'd been able to hang the laundry out on the line.

The women on his street had been terribly amused by his labors. More than one had come on the pretext of seeing if he wanted any help, but more likely to see what he was up to. Luckily, they'd brought gifts of pies and bread and a casserole, too. He'd spent several nights with a full stomach, being thankful for nosy neighbors.

Though everyone seemed to take his domestic endeavors in stride, a few of the ladies looked a bit shocked, he supposed. They weren't used to seeing a man so at home with a box of laundry detergent.

He had learned to let go of the idea that there were chores for only men or women. His time in Nicaragua had proven to him that the Lord needed everyone to do all chores, not only the things they were comfortable with.

Now, though, he had a nice fire in the

fireplace, was sipping hot tea in his father's old easy chair, and reading an old mystery novel of his father's. Gretta was snug in her bed by his feet, her head under the covers, back legs and tail slanting slightly off to one side. He felt comfortable and warm. Secure, too.

Which was an unusual thing, he realized. For the first time, he didn't ache for the way things used to be. For once, he felt like there was a chance that he could move forward in his life instead of wishing for the past.

His mission work had done far more for him than he'd ever expected. He'd gained strength and knowledge from the men and women he'd tried to help in Nicaragua. They'd reminded him about what was important. And doing without so much had taught him to adapt.

And while his time away had done so much good, he was beginning to wonder if he'd left for the right reasons. Had he only been trying to run from home when he'd told Mr. Cross and the rest of the folks at CAMA that he yearned to be sent somewhere far away for mission work? When he'd said he'd wanted to minister to the needy in other areas of the world, had that only been a part of his goals?

Instead, had he been eager to go to another country for selfish reasons? And had he returned for selfish reasons? Of course he'd wanted to see his father. But maybe he'd wanted to ease his guilt, too.

And maybe, just maybe, he'd been eager to hear praise from his father and neighbors and friends? If he was honest, he had to admit that there had been a part of him that wanted to feel special, because he'd been brave enough, tough enough, to travel far to do good works.

Instead of concentrating on the people he'd served, and how everything he'd done was God's will, he'd donned a cloak of pride and insecurity, too.

Which wasn't a good thing. Not at all.

If that was the case, Ed realized he had a lot more growing up to do. He was going to need to find a way to come to terms with the fact that Viola was right. He was completely, selfishly focused only on himself. Under the guise of helping others.

He closed the book and closed his eyes. And did something he realized he needed to do a whole lot more often. He prayed.

And then he breathed deep, let his body relax.

And prayed some more.

Viola couldn't believe what she'd just agreed to. When she'd arrived at Daybreak, she'd practically run into Edward as he was exiting the building. She was so surprised to see the man who had dominated her thoughts all weekend, she'd somehow agreed to have lunch with him today. But how could she? Besides the fact it would cause speculation among the residents, she didn't want to get to know him any better. He was only here for a short time, and . . .

The loud knock of knuckles on the cheery table next to her jarred her out of her musings. "Girly, what am I going to do with you?"

She started at the sharp rap. "Mr. Swartz, you're going to get in trouble if you keep doing that."

"Sometimes, a man has no choice in the matter."

Fidgeting under his accusing gaze, she

tried to make amends. "I'm sorry, Mr. Swartz. What have I done wrong?"

"You're ignoring me."

"Truly?" She'd brought him coffee. Had listened to all the latest gossip about the other residents.

"I've been waiting for you to ask me all about Saturday's trip to the cheese shop. But instead of thinking about me, you're looking out into the distance like a spaniel on the hunt."

"Spaniel?"

"She's a bit different from a good hunting dog, Atle," Mr. Showalter commented with a grin. "Plus, you're out of practice talking to womenfolk. They don't like men comparing them to animals."

"Jacob, you've been a widower longer than me. Maybe you've forgotten what women want to hear."

"I don't think so. At least, I might have forgotten what they want, but I definitely haven't forgotten what they don't want to hear. My wife made sure of that."

"My *frau* was a good woman. She never had any complaints."

"That may be true. But perhaps I was a better husband."

"He's got you there, Atle!" a lady sitting on the other side of the fireplace said.

Viola hid a smile as Mr. Swartz shifted, looking embarrassed. Around them, the other men and women in the room began to discuss all the lessons they'd learned over their years of marriage.

Fortified with coffee, a cozy fire, and no place to go, the conversation grew louder and more ribald, with the men easily offering one another a variety of well-placed put-downs.

Usually, such talk would burn her ears, but Viola couldn't help but chuckle at the audacity of the conversation. Her home had been closely monitored at all times for inappropriate talk and behavior. It was refreshing to be around so many people who weren't used to so many restrictions.

But that didn't mean she felt able to join in, of course. She kept her hands busy with some place cards she was organizing for a future dinner. But she listened attentively with her bright red ears.

"Daed!" Ed chided as he walked into the room. "You shouldn't be talking like that. There are ladies present."

Viola popped her head up as the rest of

the room went silent. What was he doing here? There were still a couple hours before it would be even close to lunchtime.

Instead of looking cowed by his son's comment, Mr. Swartz merely brushed off the scolding with a careless wave of his hand. "There's nothing we're saying that they haven't heard before."

"I doubt that."

"Are you offended and upset, Viola?"

"*Nee,* Mr. Swartz. I think I'm used to your way of speaking by now."

Almost comically, Atle raised his eyebrows. "See? Everything is *gut* here. Don't tell me that mission work has stunted your sense of humor, son."

Edward looked a bit affronted. "My sense of humor hasn't gone walking, Daed. It's more like your manners have."

"Some would say talking back to your poor father who's stuck in a wheelchair ain't good manners, either, Edward."

His son opened his mouth, then shut it slowly as his lips, too, curved up a bit. "You're right, Father."

Mr. Showalter chuckled, and several others suddenly became busy with their coffee and snacks.

And Viola smiled. She was torn between being embarrassed that he'd pointed out her presence, and a little miffed that he'd spoiled his father's harmless chatter.

But then Edward glanced her way. And those blue eyes froze everything that had been on the tip of her tongue.

"Viola, what time would you like to go to lunch today?"

All at once, she felt everyone's gaze fasten on her with the tenacity of a creeping vine on an ash tree.

"What's this?" Mr. Swartz asked. "I didn't know you two were courting."

"I merely asked Viola here if she'd like to share a meal with me," Ed said patiently.

"Ah," Mr. Showalter said. "A romance."

Others in the suddenly crowded-feeling room mumbled in agreement. And with each comment, it felt as if Viola's skin turned a different shade of red.

Oh, but this was terrible! This was just what she was hoping to avoid. "Mr. Showalter, this . . . this is not a romance," she blurted. "It is only a meal."

"*Jah,*" Ed said. "It's only a meal. Don't make it more than it is."

"In my day, asking a lady to share a meal

was courtship," Atle said. "Not that I'm complaining. I'm glad you have come to your senses and are takin' a shine to Viola here."

She'd now gone from blushing to wishing she could scoot out of the room.

But Ed simply crossed his arms over his chest and returned his father's sass easily. "Daed, in your day, I imagine your father knew better than to comment on your activities. Somehow, I can't imagine that Grandpa Joseph was as into your business as you seem to be in mine."

As Atle squirmed, Viola chuckled. "He's got you there, Mr. Swartz."

"Perhaps."

She glanced Ed's way, intending to share a smile. But as she did, she stilled. He was staring at her in a new way. Not heated, exactly. But with a new, fresh awareness.

Her lips parted as she felt an unexpected pull. She was attracted to him; she couldn't deny it.

Not that that was a good thing. They were far too different, and he was leaving. For a split second, she let her impatience get the best of her all over again. Only she would start liking the one man she shouldn't in Berlin.

Then, conscious of everyone's attention, she shook off her regrets. "Edward, what time would you like to eat? I can be flexible."

"Around noon?"

"You can go earlier if you want," his *daed* said.

"That's okay," Ed replied with a grin. "I wanted to spend some time with you first. Nobody's teased me since last time I was here."

His *daed* grumbled, but Viola could tell he was pleased. She stood up. "I think that's my cue to move on. I've got some other things I need to do before lunch." She held up the place cards she'd just finished writing names on. "The least of which is to put these in a safe place."

"But you'll come back to fetch Edward?"

Now it was Edward's turn to be the focus of much amusement in the room. His cheeks flushed, but to his credit, he stayed silent.

"Ed, how about you meet me in the lobby at noon?"

"That sounds good. I'll be waiting for you in the lobby at noon."

He sounded so certain. Almost like he was eager for their date!

Viola turned away before either man could see the broad smile that threatened to erupt. But before she left the room, she could hear the other residents teasing Edward about having a date.

And how, although they all teased him, he never corrected them.

After Viola left the room—and everyone got tired of teasing him—Edward and his father settled into easy conversation. They talked about his father's trip to the cheese shop, and about one of his friends who'd recently passed away.

His father asked him about the house and if he'd shoveled the sidewalk and if he'd remembered that the back door stuck in the cold.

As the minutes passed and his father's reminders continued, Ed was starting to feel as if he'd become ten years younger since he'd returned home. In Nicaragua, he'd been respected. His opinion valued. Men and women alike had depended on him for advice, and had admired his hard work ethic.

He'd had to grow up fast. He'd made some impressive mistakes and had to bear the burden of fixing his messes all by himself.

Now, though, it was starting to feel like he had never left home. Not only was his *daed* interested in his love life, but he seemed to have forgotten that he was a grown man.

For a moment, he considered speaking to his father about that, but decided against it. There was no point in it, after all. In six months he'd be gone again.

Suddenly, he felt empty.

"Tell me about the house, Edward. Does anything need to be repaired? Do you need to hire someone to come in and help you clean it better?"

"I think I got the cleaning under control." Briefly, he described his new close relationship with the bottle of Pine-Sol. Then, before he knew it, he was telling his father about the little dog who had wandered into his life. How they had enjoyed a few quiet moments together in front of the fireplace the evening before.

"That's a good spot. I've spent plenty of days in that chair myself, son."

"It's not too late, Daed. How about you move back in with me for the next six months?"

"Until you leave again?" Some of the spunk ebbed from his demeanor. "I think not."

"But it will be just like old times."

"Ah, that's where you are wrong. Nothing is ever like old times, I'm afraid. It's never the same."

"It could still be good, though. I'd love to live there with you."

"I appreciate you saying that, but this is where I belong, Edward." A faint shadow of a secret slid into his expression. "It's where I need to stay, too. I'm happy here."

Ed had a feeling his father was being completely honest. "I'm glad you're happy."

"Something that would make me mighty happy is if you continued your courtship of Miss Viola."

"I'm taking her to lunch, Daed. That's all."

"Lunch can grow to something more."

"We both know it shouldn't. I'll be leaving in six months."

"Six months is time enough to fall in love."

"Daed—"

"Don't some missionaries travel with their wives?" he interrupted.

"*Jah,* but I think you're getting a little ahead of yourself."

"Maybe so, but whether we are talking about Viola or another woman, I think it's something to think about." He eyed Ed intently through his lenses. "Promise me you'll keep an open mind."

"I'll do my best," he said dryly. What he didn't want to share was the feeling that he'd already had about Viola. He'd always wanted a woman in his life who wasn't afraid to speak her mind.

But that aside, he wasn't even sure Viola would want a life built around mission work. As it was, he and Viola had hardly had more than a handful of conversations, each one barely less stilted than the previous one. To go from lunch to asking her out for another date was a big enough step. Marriage and traveling together for mission work felt like too much of a gap to even contemplate.

Why was his father so intent on getting him hitched?

A slow steady note of worry threaded through him. "Hey, Daed? Is there something going on with you that I'm not aware of? Are you sick?"

"Certainly not."

But his father wasn't looking at him. In fact, he seemed to be doing everything he possibly could to avoid meeting Edward's gaze. "Are you sure?"

"As sure as I am that your pesky questions are beginning to annoy me, Edward. I've been living fine here in Berlin without your constant interfering. You needn't begin fussing over me now."

"I'm not fussing." Feeling more confused by the second, he looked around the room for some support. Surely there was someone nearby who could give him a hint of what was going on with his *daed*?

But during their spurious exchange, the room had emptied. Now, it was only the two of them in the big room. "Daed, are you supposed to be somewhere?"

Looking as if he were visibly holding on to the last of his patience, his father narrowed his eyes. "Why do you ask?"

"No one else is here." He stood and moved behind his father's wheelchair, and took the handles. "Would you like me to wheel you to wherever you need to go?"

"I am not an invalid, Edward!"

He let go of the wheelchair handles and stepped backward. "I know."

"Good. Now stop getting into my business."

In a lot of ways, Ed was his father's son. It went against his nature to rely on others, or to be bossed around. He kept his temper with effort. "All right."

Now that he'd won whatever sort of battle he'd been waging, his father held up a crossword puzzle with a shaky hand—the only sign, as far as Ed could see, that he, too, had been disturbed by their angry exchange of words. "Now, it's time to put that brain of yours to good use, Edward. Help me finish this puzzle."

There was only one thing to do. Ed sat back down and plucked a pencil from the holder in the center of the circular table and leaned forward. "Which clue are you working on?"

"Two across. A four-letter word for stubborn."

DAED fit the bill. But he tried for something a little less inflammatory. "How about mule? I think that might work."

After a moment, his father wrote that in. "It works, indeed."

chapter nine

They'd been walking in silence since they left the retirement home. Though Viola wasn't a woman who needed constant chatter, the awkward tension between them was so different from their usual bantering that her nerves were starting to get the best of her.

"Was it something I said?" Viola joked.

"I don't follow."

She noticed that he neither slowed his pace nor looked her way. "I'm not surprised," she said. "You've hardly looked my way for two blocks. And, you're walking so fast I practically have to jog to keep up with you."

Immediately, his steps slowed. "I'm sorry. And as for looking your way . . ." A muscle in his cheek twitched. "Did you want me staring at you?"

"Of course not. All I meant was that we've hardly spoken ten words to each other since we left the retirement home," she explained as they stepped around a woman strolling with her basset hound. "Plus, every time I've tried to start a conversation, you've looked distracted. Since this lunch was your idea, I was wondering if I've done something to upset you. Or, did you change your mind and not know how to back out of it?"

Immediately, he looked pained. "Viola, I promise, that's not it at all."

"Then what is it? Or am I just imagining things?"

"It's . . . nothing." He paused, looking as if he was tempted to say more, but instead turned and looked straight ahead again. "But no, you're not imagining things."

It would be good manners to let the matter drop. But he looked so pained, so in need of a friend, she pushed a bit. "Now we both know it's not nothing. Would you like to talk about it?"

Again, whether or not to answer her seemed like it was a monumental decision. "Maybe."

"Is it about your *daed*? Or your job?" She grasped at straws. "Is there a problem with your *haus*?"

His steps slowed right in front of one of the many gift stores that dotted the area. "It's many things, if you want to know the truth. I realized last night that I might not have come to terms with my mother's death like I had believed I had." He hung his head. "And though it shames me to admit this to you, I half feel like you were right all along."

"Right about what?"

"Maybe I really did go to Nicaragua for selfish reasons. Maybe I went down there, thinking I was going to make all these great changes, help all these people, but what really happened was that I was only thinking about myself. I wanted to get away from hurting."

Viola was shocked. Ed was speaking so honestly about things that she'd never imagined, and she felt guilty. She'd been just as self-centered as he had been, but she hadn't had the nerve to admit it to him—or even herself!

But before she could say anything, Ed sighed and started walking again. "I'm starting to worry about my *daed,* too," he said as they continued walking.

"Your father? I think he is doing well, Edward."

"Mentally? I agree. But I'm afraid his physical health isn't near as good as he pretends it is. I'm afraid he's keeping things from me, and that makes me worried."

He inhaled, as if he was expecting her to brush off his worries. Or worse, that she was going to point out that he had no right to make such judgments because he'd been gone for two years.

She felt his wariness as if it were her own. And yet again, she felt embarrassed for how judgmental she'd been.

But that wouldn't ease his mind. He clearly wanted to talk about his father, so she nodded seriously. "I would have heard if the medical staff had worries about him."

"You think so?"

"I know so. Everyone at Daybreak keeps a good eye on the residents. But that doesn't mean that you're wrong. What have you noticed? What seems off?"

"I'm not sure, exactly." He shrugged. "Like I said, it's just a feeling, and it's probably nothing." Then, preferring to get her criticisms out in the open, he added, "Here you've been giving me grief about being away from my *daed*. I hadn't thought you were right. But maybe you were. Perhaps I should never have left. I can't expect everyone else to keep a close eye on him."

Now that he was saying she was right, she'd never felt more wrong. They were in front of the Johnson's hardware store now, almost to the pizza parlor. As she glanced into the shop's windows, she saw that the owners still hadn't changed their Christmas display.

Which reminded her of the way she'd thought about Edward. Before she'd met him, she'd thought he was a careless son, off gallivanting around the world while his father had to make friends with strangers. But now that she'd met him . . . "I judged you without even really knowing you, Ed. That was wrong of me."

"Maybe you weren't that off the mark."

"*Nee,* I was hasty to judge. It was wrong.

And as far as feeling like you're running away, well, I think we all run away from our hurts, to some extent."

"I don't think we all run to another country."

"Maybe you were running away, but you did good work there! You did something to be proud of. Everyone grieves, but not everyone is willing to help other people while grieving."

His eyes widened, as if she'd really surprised him. "Thank you for saying that. I never looked at it that way. How did you get so smart?"

"I don't feel smart at all. As a matter of fact, I've been feeling a lot of the same things that you've been feeling. That I was going along in my life, serving others, but really simply keeping myself happy." Now that she was baring her soul, she felt compelled to continue, even if it didn't paint her in the best light. "Ed, I've been learning lately that appearances can be deceiving. Mighty deceiving."

"Now I feel like I'm the one who needs to be coaxing information out of you. Are you having troubles, too? Is something going on with your family?"

"Yes. I mean, no." When she spied his look of confusion, she sought to explain a bit. "I mean, I'm fine, but there are some things that are happening in my family that I'm . . . upset about."

"You know you sound terribly awkward, don'tcha?"

"*Jah*," she said sheepishly.

"Shall we go inside, then?" He opened the door to the pizzeria.

"Sure. I'd rather focus on pizza than on my problems."

"I, as well." As he approached the hostess stand, he sniffed the air appreciatively. "It smells like heaven in here. I don't know if pizza will help our worries, but I have a feeling that it can't hurt. I haven't had a slice of pizza in ages."

Seeing the pure enjoyment on his face, just from the thought of pizza, made Viola realize that she'd never really taken the time to think about all he'd given up when he moved away. "You had to make do with all kinds of changes, living far away, didn't you?"

"I did." When the hostess greeted them, he held up two fingers before continuing as they followed her to a booth. "Most things

I didn't miss. I learned to like many of the foods in Nicaragua, like empanadas and rice and beans and tortillas. But there were some things that couldn't be replaced. A thick slice of pepperoni pizza from Pizza Palace is one of them."

After they were seated and ordered two waters, Viola chuckled. "That's something, don't you think? An Amish man wasn't missing roasted chicken, but pizza."

He grinned. "I'm Amish, but not an Amish saint, Viola. I've never been one to ignore the calling of a thick slice of pepperoni and mushroom pizza."

She wrinkled her nose. "We don't have to have mushrooms on our pizza, do we?"

"We don't have to do anything you don't want to do," he said softly.

She knew that he was referring to much more than how she liked her pizza. The look in his eyes was an invitation for more. For more of a relationship, more dates, more time spent together. And that would have been all well and good, if he wasn't leaving in six months.

"I'll take any kind of pizza you want," she said, keeping things light. "I'll even pick off mushrooms if you really want them."

"I had no idea you were so agreeable."

"I'm usually not. You must have caught me on an off day."

"I think your off days might be my blessings. Tell me, do you get in an agreeable mood often?"

"Most would say not often enough."

Their banter continued over a pizza loaded with enough sausage and vegetables and pepperoni that Viola had to use a knife and fork to eat her piece neatly.

They chatted about everything and nothing. Without either of them saying it, both of them were eager to brush off serious conversation and focus on things that didn't matter.

They talked about foods they liked and the times of year they hated. She entertained him with stories about being a twin, and he told her tales of playing baseball after church with his friends. And in the midst of their laughter, they both realized that meaningless conversation wasn't meaningless after all.

It was good to be able to laugh and relax together. Neither wanted to take every moment of every day too seriously.

And then, all too soon, it was time to go.

"It's after two. I'm sorry I kept you here so long," he said, eyeing the clock.

"I can't believe we were here two hours."

"Time flies, for sure."

When they got back out on the sidewalk, he buttoned up his coat while she wrapped a thick wool scarf more securely around her neck. "Where are you off to now? You're done with work today, right?"

"I am. My aunt Lorene lives nearby. I'm going over to her house to bake cookies. We're hosting church this weekend, so there's lots to do to get ready. I need to be available for my sister, and for my *mamm,* too, in case anything else falls apart in the *haus.*"

"Do you need some help? I could stop by sometime this week. Other than visiting my father, I don't have a lot going on."

"There's no need. But thank you."

"Are you working tomorrow?"

"I am."

"Then I'll look for you then, Viola. Thank you for having lunch with me."

Viola smiled before turning away.

"Viola?"

She stopped and turned to look back at him. "Yes?"

"Would you . . . Would you want to go to lunch again soon?"

"I would." There was no reason to be coy.

He grinned. "Great. I'll talk to you about it tomorrow."

After waving a hand at him, she turned back around and picked up her pace. Thinking about his smile, her body warmed with happiness. He'd asked her out again, and she'd accepted!

But as she stopped at an intersection, nerves and doubts got ahold of her again. Once she'd agreed to this lunch date, she'd hoped that it would prove to her that he was not the man for her. But instead of that happening, she'd discovered that they were able to talk easily about most any topic. They could banter, and then switch gears and begin to share meaningful thoughts and concerns.

And even more, she appreciated his ability to put his imperfections in God's hands, and to be guided by Him. For the first time, Viola considered adopting that way of thinking. It would feel so good to let someone else take control of her life. To put her faith and worries and fears into someone else's hands.

chapter ten

Lovina had always preferred to sit at the kitchen table instead of in the *sitzschtupp*, the good living room, when she was alone. Years ago, Aaron had ceased asking her the why of it. He liked to sit in his thick easy chair. It felt better on his back, and he liked the way the cushions curved around his sides.

But she liked the sturdiness of the hard ladder-back chair against her spine, and the way the scarred, smooth oak felt under her hands. Sitting at the head of the table made her recall other days. Better days. The days of serving breakfast to six scrubbed faces every morning before her busy children went off to school. When she'd have women over to help with a quilt, or write down recipes for a new bride.

Of course, she also had memories of her mama's kitchen table. Back when she was in high school, she used to do her homework at the kitchen table. Her mother would give her a Coke and read the paper or talk on the phone while she struggled through conjugating French verbs. Or her history homework. Or geometry. Boy had she hated geometry!

She'd been sitting at one almost just like this when Jack had asked her to go to the homecoming dance with him. She still remembered how handsome he'd been, his hair damp from his shower after football practice . . . a bruise on his cheek that she'd fussed over. He'd blushed from all her attention.

She'd thought she was in love.

Leaning back, in the quiet of her kitchen, where no one was around to see . . . Lovina allowed herself to smile. He'd been so nervous when he'd asked her to the dance. Jack Kilgore, one of the most pop-ular boys in her class!

She'd tried to play it cool, but inside, she'd been so giddy and excited, she'd hardly been able to stand it. No doubt she hadn't fooled him for a second.

"Lolly, will you go to the dance with me? I promise, it will be a great time."

She remembered thinking that she should be coy. Maybe tell him that she wanted to think about it for a day or two. But all those ideas had flown out the window. Instead, she'd beamed like she was the happiest girl in the world. "I'd love to, Jack," she'd said.

Then he'd reached out and squeezed her hand. Just once.

Lovina glanced down at her hand, now red and rough and lined with age and years of hard work. For a brief moment, all she saw was smooth, creamy skin and neatly filed nails. Her hand had looked so small in his. It had looked perfect.

She'd run to the phone the minute he'd left and called up all her best girlfriends. They'd giggled and squealed and oohed when she'd described how his hand had felt on hers.

And not a one of them had thought she

was crazy when she'd admitted that she wasn't going to wash it for days. . . .

"Mamm?"

With a start, she saw Peter standing in the doorway. Bringing in with him the present.

Clenching her hand, she hid it under her apron, as if it might give away her thoughts. Abruptly, she got to her feet. "What do you want?"

His look of concern vanished to barely concealed irritation. "I told Marie I'd ask if you wanted to help with the tablecloths today."

Ever since Marie and Peter had moved into the main house, she'd continued to help iron and lay out the tablecloths. No one else did it right. Even though it was only Monday, Lovina felt sure that her daughter-in-law was running around in a panic. Getting a *haus* ready to host church was a lot of work.

But after twenty years of ironing tablecloths, she didn't feel like doing it.

"Marie can do the tablecloths this time. I'm going to stay here."

After studying her for a long moment,

Peter turned on his heel and walked out. Not bothering to ask if she was all right, or why she'd changed her mind after years of being the one in charge of the proper care of their tables.

Actually, she realized with some dismay, he was acting just the way she'd taught him to act. The way she'd taught all her children to be. Dutiful. Respectful.

When the door closed, she leaned back in her chair and sighed. She'd made a great many mistakes in her life. She'd been too critical with her children. Too formal with her husband. Too distant with her grand-children.

But those mistakes were nothing com-pared to the mistakes she'd made her senior year in high school.

Just as nothing had been as sweet as her first dance with Jack.

Closing her eyes, she coaxed her brain to turn back to that wonderful, carefree time. Back when she'd rolled her hair in pin curls and then fastened the hard-won ringlets back with bows.

Thought about the white gloves and the strapless pink dress. About her red lipstick and the blue eye shadow.

And how she'd felt when she'd slow-danced in Jack's arms. And even though later that night everything had fallen apart, that dance had been so special.

Magical. So much so that hardly anything had matched it since. As she remembered the music that played and the way her satin dress had felt against her nylon-covered calves, she smiled.

She rarely gave in to weakness and let herself think back to those days.

But today? Today she was going to live in the past.

There was a message waiting on Edward's home phone when he glanced at it after walking back from Daybreak.

"Edward! This is James Cross," the familiar voice boomed in his ear. "I hope you're having a good time being back in Berlin, and are enjoying your visit with your father." He paused. "Listen, something's come up and I wanted to talk to you about it. How does your schedule look next Tuesday? Can you stop by the office? I'd like to speak to you in person, if I may. Let me know. Oh, and let me know if you'd like someone to pick you up. We'd be glad to arrange that." Mr. Cross closed the message with both the office and his cell phone number.

Well, that was unexpected.

Since Ed had the office phone number already memorized, he called there first. "Edward Swartz here," he told the assistant who answered. "Is Mr. Cross available?"

"Hi, Ed. This is Michele. Mr. Cross isn't in, but he did want me to ask what time you can come in next Tuesday. Do you have a time that's convenient for you?"

"How about nine in the morning?"

"Nine will work for him. I've penciled that in. Do you need a ride?"

"Thanks. That would be great."

"All right then." Ed heard Michele click a couple of keys on her computer. "Are you still at the same address?"

"I am."

"Okay. Looks like Jared Schilling can pick you up at eight fifty next Tuesday morning. Will that work?"

Mr. Schilling was one of the directors. "That will be fine with me," he said dryly.

"I think we're all set. See you—"

"Hey," he said quickly, before Michele

hung up. "Do you know what this is all about?"

"I think Mr. Cross would rather be the person to talk to you about this."

"Can you at least tell me if I'm in trouble?"

Michele chuckled softly. "You're not in trouble, Ed. Don't worry about that."

"All right. Thanks. I'll see you next week." When he hung up, he couldn't help but wonder what reason they could have for meeting with him. There might be some questions about the mission in Nicaragua. Or they could be asking if he could do some office work while he was living in Berlin.

But at the edge of his mind was the slim possibility that they wanted to talk about another job for him. What if they wanted to send him out again sooner than later?

What if it was to someplace even farther away, such as one of the mission sites in Africa?

Before he came home, he would have accepted any appointment without hesitation. He would have believed that God had put the opportunity in front of him, and that he needed to be mindful of that.

But now he wasn't so sure.

Perhaps God had placed him back in Berlin for a very special reason. To be with his father, to rescue Gretta, to find his home again . . . and to meet Viola.

Was he willing to say goodbye to so much just as he was finally learning to say hello to it all?

chapter eleven

"Lovina doesn't want to iron the table-cloths?" Marie asked, dismay rich in her voice.

"I'm afraid not."

"Why not? What in the world is she doing?"

Peter thought about sharing the truth. About how he'd found his mother sitting at her kitchen table, staring at her hands like they were new attachments to her body. But twenty-some-odd years of marriage had brought him wisdom. If he shared that, it would only heighten the tension between his wife and his mother. "She looks a bit under the weather. Matter of fact, I wouldn't be surprised if she was taking a nap right now."

"Your mother is napping in the middle of the afternoon?" Looking concerned, she dropped the tablecloths onto the couch and looked at the door that led to the *dawdi haus* with apprehension. "Do you think I should go visit her?"

That was the thing about Marie. She didn't like barging in on his mother, not after living with her for more than twenty years.

But if it was the right thing to do, she would do it, always. That was simply the kind of person she was.

They both knew his mother wasn't the type of woman to appreciate Marie prying into her personal business. And experience told him that his mother was in just enough of a mood to say something regrettable to his wife. "*Nee!* I mean, no. I think we should let her take her rest. You know I didn't get much information. She could be feeling under the weather for any variety of reasons. We don't want to embarrass her."

"I suppose you're right."

He patted his wife's shoulder. "I know I am. Let's leave her alone for now." He picked up one of the tablecloths. "I could help you, if you want. I have time to iron."

She snatched the white cloth from his hands. "I think not. You'll only make things worse."

He'd been hoping she'd say that. In their twenty years of marriage, he'd yet to pick up an iron, and he was hoping to keep things that way.

The next morning, Peter joined Roman at the woodpile in the back of the barn.

Ax already in hand, Roman straightened when he approached. "Daed? What are you doing here?"

"Thought I'd help you chop wood." At his son's look of dismay, Peter interjected a touch of humor in his tone. "I think the exercise might do these old muscles of mine some good."

Roman pressed his right hand to the back of his neck—the telltale sign that he was irritated.

But, as he was apt to do, he kept his silence.

Breaking up the tension, Peter pointed to the stump a few yards to Roman's left. "I'll work over there, out of your way."

After staring at the stump for a moment, his son shrugged. "All right, Daed." He turned then, stretched his arms a bit, then swung the ax in a smooth arc over his shoulder.

The log it connected with split easily with a crisp *crack.*

Almost immediately, Roman reached for another piece of wood, placed it on the stump, and swung again.

Peter's process went far slower. It had been years since he'd split logs, and the lack of practice showed. His muscles were screaming after only five swings of the ax.

But still he continued.

After another ten minutes, Peter was longing for a hot shower.

He decided to break the silence. "Roman, I came out here to see if you wanted to talk about anything."

Roman's rhythm never slowed. "I don't."

Peter set his ax down. "You sure? I know there's been lots going on."

"Mighty sure." Crack went the ax again. Finally, his boy stopped and stood up straight. "It's all been said, don'tcha think?"

Roman's statement wasn't much of a surprise. His son seemed to be happiest keeping a bit of distance from them all. But in this case, he was also right. "I suppose it has all been said," he murmured quietly.

Roman nodded, then reached for another log.

Peter couldn't bear the thought of lifting that ax again. Rubbing his shoulders, he shrugged. "Um, I think I've chopped enough wood for one day."

Roman's lips curved slightly. "You might be right about that."

Peter chuckled to himself as he made his way back to the house. After putting away his ax, he went into the kitchen and washed up. Then, before Marie could ask why he'd been chopping wood, he held up her grocery list. "I'm going to go talk to Sam and take care of your shopping."

"*Danke,* Peter."

He harnessed Star and set out for town. Usually, Sam and his wife, Mary Beth, liked to eat lunch in town on Tuesdays. It gave them a chance to enjoy a meal together—a rare thing with three busy children. With any luck, he'd find them easily and they could have a few minutes to discuss what to do about their mother.

Besides the shocking news last week,

he was starting to get the feeling that something wasn't right with her.

When he pulled into the wide parking lot of the Farmstead Restaurant, he spied his older brother and his wife just entering the large building.

Ten minutes later, he had hitched Star up to the post, ordered a sandwich, and was sitting across from them in one of the booths in the cozy home-style restaurant.

"I wondered if we'd see you today," Sam said. "How are things at home?"

"About what you'd expect," he said dryly. "Between church and Mamm's news, it's chaotic."

"Tell Marie that I've made apricot bars," Mary Beth said. "Two batches of them."

"I'm sure she'll be most grateful."

Sam leaned back. "Do you want to talk about our meeting the other night?"

Peter shuddered. "I'd say yes if I thought it would do any good. I'm still reeling about Lorene's secret love for John Miller. You're closer to her than I am. Did you have any idea all that happened?"

Sam shook his head. "None."

"I saw her this morning," Mary Beth said. "She still seems pretty broken up about it."

"I wonder what really happened?"

Sam shrugged. "Who knows? It all happened years ago. There's nothing we can do about it."

"We could go talk to John. . . ."

"And say what? I'm sure he's moved on. He's probably married by now."

"He's not," Mary Beth said.

Peter turned to her in surprise. "You know him?"

"I know of him."

"Well, all I care about is Mamm and Daed finally coming clean about how they got together. Until we get that settled, it feels like the whole family is going to fall apart," Peter said, taking a large gulp of his water.

After a quick glance Mary Beth's way, Sam said, "Perhaps we need to face the truth, Peter. There's nothing we can do about the past. And there's nothing we can do about our parents and their secrets. They obviously have reasons for keeping what happened a secret from their children. Maybe they should have their privacy."

"But this is our family."

"That's true, but just because we're related doesn't mean we can't have private lives."

"I just have the feeling that our parents have only told us half the story."

"They haven't really told us anything! If there is more to the story, I hope I never find out about it!" his brother quipped. "Knowing Mamm grew up English has been quite enough."

Peter wanted to be agreeable. And he certainly didn't want to go borrowing any more trouble. But privately, he wasn't sure that letting the past slide was the best course of action.

You have secrets, too, his conscience reminded him darkly.

He cleared his throat. "Um, now that I think about it, I do agree that it's best to let the past lie. There's no reason to shake things up more than they already are."

"I'm glad we're all in agreement," Sam said with a satisfied smile. "Now, shall we pray, before our food arrives?"

"Of course," Mary Beth said.

They all bowed their heads in silent prayer. When they raised their heads, there seemed to be a calmer feeling among them all.

Prayer always had a way of doing that,

Peter realized. He needed to pray for strength and guidance more often.

But even with that in mind, Peter found himself thinking about Sam's statement about their need for private lives.

He sure hoped a certain part of his life stayed private.

"Gretta, here we are again," Ed said when he walked into the quiet house shortly after noon.

The little dog yipped a bit, circling his heels. After he knelt down to scratch behind her ears, she wagged her tail and followed him into the kitchen, looking expectant all the while.

"Lunchtime, is it?" he said with a smile. "Luckily, I bought you some dog food." He poured her about a half-cup's worth, then chuckled to himself as he went back to the bag he'd left outside the front door and brought it inside, too. He pulled out a rawhide chew, squeaky dog toy, collar, and leash from the bag.

When the dog finished her dinner, he presented her with his purchases, just as if she were a child instead of a tiny stray.

She held her neck still while he fastened the collar, as though she were receiving a shiny diamond necklace.

Instantly, Gretta picked up the squeaky bear and trotted off, her tail wagging so fast that it was a blur.

What was happening to him? He probably shouldn't even have taken the dog in, let alone begun buying treats for her. He was leaving in six months' time. Viola was right. Who would care for the dog then?

But somehow, he hadn't been able to resist making the dog happy. Fussing over her did his heart a world of good.

Just as he didn't seem to be able to resist spending time with Viola Keim.

Today he'd only gotten the chance to see her for a few moments. She'd had business in another part of the building and his father had wanted to listen to a guest speaker with him.

Though he'd enjoyed spending time with his father, Ed had found his mind drifting more than once while the environmentalist talked. He couldn't wait to ask her out again.

Couldn't wait to see her smile.

Which, like buying a stray dog toys, was probably not a good idea.

Though he didn't need the reminder—it was clear in his mind—he said out loud, "She is not for you, Edward. Her life is here, yours is not. Plus, she's terribly opinionated, which isn't necessarily the best quality to have when one is a missionary's wife. Why, sometimes I think she's got herself perched on such a high horse that it's a wonder she hasn't fallen off its back."

He half expected the Lord to say something right back to him—remind him that it wasn't terribly Christian to be talking about Viola like he was.

But all that happened was Gretta wagged her tail and tilted her head at him. He laughed. "You are the perfect listener, dog. You always find a way to look terribly interested, yet you don't offer a bit of unwanted advice." If only there were more humans like that in the world.

Still musing on his relationship with Viola, he turned on a few lights and washed out the two plates he'd left in the sink after breakfast.

That chore done, he picked up the stack of mail he'd retrieved from the post office that morning. There were two letters from friends in Nicaragua, a few bills to be paid, and an official-looking letter from the head of the agency.

He practically jumped when he heard a knock at the door.

When he opened it, he found John Miller standing on the other side. John had been their neighbor when Ed was in grade school. A few years after that, his family moved to the other side of Berlin. John was Old Order Amish, and was a good ten years older. But since Ed had never had any siblings, he'd been sad to lose the only playmate he'd ever known.

"John! What a sight for sore eyes you are!"

John lifted his eyebrows but didn't tease him about his exuberance. "I'm glad to see you, too."

"What brings you by?"

"I took off early from the store and decided to see if the rumor about you being home was true."

Ed grinned. "It's true," he said as he clasped his old friend's hand.

"You look *gut*. How are you?"

"I don't hardly know anymore, if you want to know the truth," he joked. "I'm still trying to get used to life back here in Ohio."

He stepped back and motioned John inside. "Come in, man. It's too cold to be chatting out here."

After a moment's hesitation, John walked through the entryway then stopped at the front of his living room—his fairly empty living room. "You need some furniture, Ed. Come by the store and I'll get you set up."

"Thanks, but I'm only here temporarily. My *daed,* you know, is living over at Daybreak. I haven't had too much time to get settled in." Though, of course, the latter was a lie. He'd had time. But he'd had little to unpack and no way to make the place more cozy. Other than Gretta, of course.

John nodded. "Makes sense, for sure. Well, if you change your mind, we've got some things in the back that are on sale."

"I appreciate that. Listen, I couldn't have been happier for you when I heard that you own Miller's Fine Furniture. My father told me it's doing real well."

"*Danke.* I feel blessed, to be sure."

"And Thomas? How is he?"

A shadow fell across his face. "He's fine, but I'm afraid I don't see much of him. He left the Order and is working in Toledo in one of those new glass factories that have sprung up."

"I'm shocked he left the Order."

"It was hard for me to accept." John shrugged. "I can understand his reasons to an extent, though. Being shuffled to our uncle wasn't easy. Uncle Clyde was Amish, but not exactly what I'd call a godly man. All Thomas ever talked about was getting away."

"And so he did."

John nodded. "Enough about me. Tell me about your work. I heard you're working for CAMA, and that they sent you out of the country."

"Yep. I was doing mission work in Nicaragua."

"That's pretty far away."

Ed chuckled. "No, that's *really* far away."

"What brought you back?"

"My time was up. Plus, I was anxious to see my father." He realized they were still standing. "I'm glad you stopped by. Want to sit down for a bit?"

"I'd be happy to." John sat, and accepted the offer of coffee, which took Ed into the kitchen briefly. While it was brewing he sat back down. "Now that you know all about me, why don't you tell me what you've been up to."

"About what you'd imagine. Now that I opened my own store, I've been busier than I could have ever dreamed."

Even in his short time of being back, Ed had heard that the business was doing very well.

He was pleased to hear an unmistakable note of pride in John's voice, too. Like most people on their street, he'd been well aware of what John's home life had been like growing up. After his mother had passed away, many in the community had watched the Miller family slowly crumble apart. "We're all proud of you, for sure."

"*Gott* has been might good to me."

"Yes, He has. You sound content."

"After the way things used to be? Yes, I am." He coughed. "More or less. How about you?"

"Oh, I'm glad to be back, and trying to fit into country life again." For a moment, Ed was tempted to tell him more. To share how stressful so much of his time in Nicaragua had been. People were hungry or sick or alone or . . . you name it. Sometimes, hearing people in Berlin complain about the cold or the noise on the street got on his nerves. Those were such small things.

He got up, poured two cups of coffee, then brought them back into the living room. "Would you like to go grab something to eat?"

"Maybe another time. Actually, Ed, there's another reason I wanted to talk to you."

"Okay . . ."

"One of the gals who works for me saw you and Viola Keim walking together yesterday. Is that true? Are you friends?"

He couldn't believe he was part of the gossip mill already. "Sure, we're friends. I mean, she works at Daybreak, and my father is very fond of her."

"Do you know her family well?"

"I don't know them at all. I merely invited her to go get some pizza with me." With effort, he pushed away the energized feeling he always got when he thought about being near her. "Why?"

"Her aunt came to see me the other day."

"And? Is there a problem?"

"Not really. Unless you count her break-ing my heart years ago."

Now if that didn't shock him, he didn't know what would. "I didn't know you and Viola's aunt were friends."

"Oh, we were more than that. I wanted to marry Lorene."

"How old is she?" he asked, trying to picture the two of them.

"Viola's got lots of aunts and uncles. Her aunt Lorene is the youngest. She's thirty-two."

"So, she's your age."

"Yep."

Ed still wasn't sure what this had to do with him.

But if he'd learned anything while out in the field, it was that less talking equaled more sharing. So, he picked an open-ended question. "How did you feel about her visit?"

"Taken aback. Kind of at a loss. Con-fused." He looked thoughtful as he contin-ued the list. "And, if you want to know the truth, more than a little angry." He rubbed his smooth chin. "That in itself caught me off guard."

"Why were you angry? I mean, ten years is a long time to hold a grudge."

He leaned back against the cushions of the old couch. "Believe me, I know it's been too long to be stewing about something that happened so long ago. But I got angry because . . . I think I still feel something for her, Ed. And I don't want to. After all this time, after all the work I've done to get over her, and to make something positive out of my life . . . she's gone and messed it up."

Jumping to his feet, Ed said, "Would you like a bit more coffee? I'll go get the carafe."

He turned away toward the kitchen without even waiting for John to respond. But his response wouldn't have mattered, anyway. What Ed needed was an excuse to buy himself some time. Because he felt suspiciously the same way about Viola. When she'd entered his life, she'd taken all his plans and mixed them up.

When he came back, John still wore a look of confusion. "What should I do? I got the feeling she wants to make amends."

"Let her, then."

"Really?"

"All of us need the chance to make things right with people we hurt. God wants that."

"You're right about that."

"And, life is short. Maybe now things will be different between you two."

A sudden hope entered his eyes. "Do you think that's possible?"

"I hope so. I'd hate to think that all of us had to give up on second chances, John."

"You're right." He straightened a bit. "I'm living proof of that."

"Indeed you are."

"I'm going to go see her at work later this week."

"I wish you the best with your visit." Ed was genuinely happy for John. And if he was a little envious, too? Well, that was something he intended to keep to himself.

Later that night, as he stoked the fire, planning to get some reading done before bed, the phone rang.

"Ed?"

Surprised to hear Viola's voice, he gripped the receiver tighter. "Viola, why are you calling?"

"Why? Oh . . . well, I just . . . uh . . . wanted to make sure you knew you were welcome to attend church at our *haus* on Sunday."

"*Danke*. That is kind of you to let me know."

"So, do you think you'll be coming?"

He recognized the hope in her voice—it was the same thing he was feeling. "I'll plan on it," he said. He couldn't help but smile into the empty room.

"I'm glad. But, ah, I should warn you that my parents will likely pepper you with questions. It's their nature to be nosy."

"It sounds like someone else I know," he teased. "I don't mind questions from you, or your parents."

She laughed. "I guess I have been letting my curiosity get the best of me. But I didn't want you to be taken off guard by my parents' nosiness."

"I promise, it won't be anything I can't handle."

"Oh. Yes, I suppose you would be used to talking about yourself with lots of people."

"It's the nature of my job." He cleared his throat. "Hey, Viola?"

"Yes?"

"I hope you and I will be able to spend some time together, too."

"Me, too." Finally, some of the uncertainty in her tone was replaced by happiness.

He was glad about that . . . because that was kind of the way he felt, too.

chapter twelve

It would have been impossible to avoid
Viola Keim at the luncheon after church.
Ed didn't even try. Everywhere he'd looked,
she flitted like a butterfly, seeming to make
sure everyone had what they needed at
the same time.

Dressed in a pale green dress that con-
trasted well with her dark hair and eyes,
she drew his gaze like little else could.

Inside the barn, next to the long tables
laden with food, Viola's parents hovered
nearby. From the time he'd arrived, he had
felt as if his every gesture toward Viola
had been watched carefully.

Ed didn't mind the scrutiny, though. He wanted to get to know Viola better . . . and that meant getting to know her family, too.

"Edward, how are you liking being back in Ohio?" her father asked politely.

"I'm enjoying it."

"And being back in your own bed?" Mr. Keim chuckled. "Whenever my wife and I go on a trip, that's always the first thing we talk about missing."

Mrs. Keim joined them. "Sometimes we miss the comfort of our own bed and pillows more than the *kinner*," she joked.

Edward grinned. "I have enjoyed being home, though to be truthful, being home doesn't have the same feeling it used to, now that I'm there by myself."

"Yes, Viola told us that your father was living over at Daybreak," Mrs. Keim said.

Ed braced himself for the criticism he was sure was about to come. But instead of sounding judgmental, both of Viola's parents looked as if they didn't find anything out of the ordinary.

"Now that I'm back, I thought my *daed* might want to move back in, but he said he likes where he is. He didn't even want to venture over here with me today. He said they have services there on Sunday that he enjoys."

"I'm afraid I would side with your father on that," Mr. Keim said. "The weather is cold, for sure. Too chilly to be going out and about if one doesn't have to."

"But we're certainly pleased you are here, Edward."

"Thank you for allowing me to worship here, even though I'm out of your church district."

"It was Viola's invitation, but we were happy you decided to join us. It's nice to have you here. Plus, we're mighty proud of you. Not everyone is called to go to other countries to spread God's word. Well, it's a blessing for sure. Ain't so, Viola?" Mrs. Keim asked as she passed by holding a tray of cookies.

"Pardon?"

After snatching a snickerdoodle cookie, her father said, "We were just telling Ed here that we are all proud of his good works."

Mrs. Keim chimed in. "And that we're glad to get to know him."

She smiled at Ed. "Me, too."

Just like that, the bond that he'd felt

over the telephone line came right back. Feeling a little like a lovesick pup, he smiled back.

When her parents conveniently excused themselves with the tray of cookies, leaving just the two of them standing together, Ed couldn't resist teasing her. "I'm impressed. You sounded almost excited about my mission work."

"You know I feel bad about how hard I was on you. My sister, Elsie, pointed that out to me. And don't forget, I've already apologized."

"It's okay. I didn't join CAMA in order to receive praise." He smiled to take the bite out of his words, then looked around the room. "Where is Elsie? I need to meet the woman who can change your mind."

Viola scanned the room. "Elsie does have a way of making me realize when I'm being shortsighted." She laughed. "Ah, there she is."

Viola led the way.

The first thing he noticed was that they weren't identical, though they had many of the same features. Brown eyes, brown hair, slim build.

"Elsie, this is Edward Swartz," Viola said when they approached her sister.

"Hi," Ed said.

Slowly, Elsie got to her feet. "It's nice to meet you," she said with a sweet smile. "I've heard a lot about you."

"Elsie," Viola warned, "you know I haven't been talking about Ed."

Looking mischievous, Elsie turned to Ed. "Please tell me about this little dog Viola said discovered you."

Next thing Ed knew, he was talking about Gretta just as if she'd been a special part of his family for years, not days.

Elsie was easy to talk to, and Viola seemed softer and more at ease by her side.

Which Ed found very interesting.

Before long, he knew it was time for him to take his leave. The majority of the church attendees had already left, and he had a feeling the Keims were ready to relax.

As he headed toward the door, he pulled Viola aside. "When will you be back at Daybreak?"

"Tomorrow."

"What time?"

Her eyes narrowed. "Why?"

"I'd like to see you. And," he added in a rush, "I thought maybe we could go out for a slice of pie this time."

"But we had lunch together twice last week." He'd impulsively asked her to a brief lunch on Thursday afternoon. She'd looked like she wanted to say no, but gave in, and they'd had a wonderful time laughing and sharing stories. He just couldn't seem to get enough of her.

"Yes, so far we've had pizza and sandwiches together. Not a single slice of pie. Not even my father's chocolate pie."

Her lips twitched.

He didn't blame her amusement; he knew he was acting a bit foolish. "Come on, Viola, say yes."

He felt her gaze on him. Measuring him. "I work at Daybreak from nine to four. If you wanted to go out for pie, it would have to be after that . . ."

"That suits me perfectly. I'll see you then, if not before. I'm sure I'll be passing the afternoon with my father and his friends— most likely losing hand after hand at cards." And trying to find a way to ask her out on a real date, in the evening.

Her cheeks bloomed. "You are too funny, Edward."

He was a lot of things. At the moment, he was smitten with Viola. Though he wasn't sure it was the best decision he'd ever made . . . and he had no idea how to stop it from happening.

In spite of all the commotion and work leading up to it, church had been wonderful. Viola had sat next to Elsie like she always did and felt the warm caress of God's guiding hand on her spirit as she prayed beside her sister. Sometimes she took having a twin for granted, but at times, like church, when they were next to each other but not saying a single word, Viola was again reminded that their bond was terribly special.

Surrounding them were their circle of friends, as well as their aunts Lorene and Mary Beth. Two rows behind them had sat her mother and grandmother. For a few hours, all the turmoil that had been brewing fell away as they focused on something far greater than all of them.

After the service was over, she'd enjoyed visiting with their many friends. And, of course, spending more time with Ed.

It had caught her a bit off guard, seeing the way he'd gotten along so well with her parents and Elsie. Perhaps that was his personality—he was a real charmer. Or maybe it was her family who'd gone out of their way to make him feel welcome. Any opportunity for a respite from the present drama unfolding in their home had been very much appreciated.

But Viola knew that there was more happening than just that. For the last two years, she'd done her best to try to make a connection with one of the eligible men in the congregation. She'd smiled and chatted. Had done her best to be interested in what they had to say.

But even as the men talked about their jobs and their farms and their families and their horses . . . she knew she'd only been going through the motions. She'd felt curiously empty. She'd felt no spark igniting, or even warmly simmering. Instead, there was an emptiness as she realized yet again that she wasn't interested.

But now, she felt different.

She didn't know what she was going to do about that.

chapter thirteen

After stewing about her feelings for Edward most of the afternoon and evening—and enduring a great amount of teasing from Elsie—Viola was especially eager to go to Daybreak on Monday morning.

She was happy to ride for once, too. Because Lorene had ended up spending the night after church, her parents were letting Viola take the buggy to work. She'd drop her aunt off on the way.

They'd just fastened their cloaks when her mother spied her down the hall.

"Viola, is it already time for you to go to work?"

"I'm afraid so."

Brow furrowed, her mother approached. "When you took this job, I never imagined that they'd want to work you so hard. Sometimes it feels like they need you most every day of the week."

"They don't make me feel that way. Mrs. Ames is a mighty charitable woman."

"Is she? Because if she was truly charitable, I would think she would hire more of you girls so you wouldn't have to work so many hours."

"I like the work, and the paychecks, too. Most days it doesn't even feel like I'm working. It feels more like I'm simply visiting with the residents."

"Viola, you're splitting hairs."

"No, I'm telling you the truth." Wearily, she glanced Lorene's way, silently begging for help.

Lorene rested a hand on her *mamm*'s shoulder. "Work can be a blessing, Marie," she murmured.

But instead of being mollified, her *mamm* continued with her questioning. "What time do you stop today?"

"Four o'clock."

"All right. I'll look for you then." Her

mother started to bustle back to the kitchen.

"Actually, Edward Swartz is taking me out for pie after work. So I'll be home after that."

Her mother swirled around, a glint in her eye. "My goodness! You're planning to see him again? So soon?"

"I see him almost every day when I work now. He likes to spend time with his father."

"Well, make sure he sees you home. It will be dark by five o'clock."

"I'll do that."

"We'd best be on our way," Lorene said. "Viola promised to take me on a little tour of Daybreak before I go home. I'm looking forward to seeing all her friends." Lorene winked.

God bless Lorene! Viola knew she'd specifically used the word *friends* to support her.

Folding her arms across her chest, her mother nodded. "Well, I suppose you two should go. The day isn't getting any shorter."

As if she hadn't been the one keeping them here!

"*Danke,* Mamm," Viola said before shutting the door. "And thank you, Lorene," she said when they were alone. "If you hadn't been here, I don't know if I would've gotten out of there without a dozen more questions."

"Anytime, dear. I promise, I know what you're going through."

Moments later, they were riding side by side in the buggy, Star easily plodding down the quiet road next to their property.

Viola held the reins easily, though part of her whimsically wondered if she even needed to do that much work. Star knew the route, and never seemed to mind the journey, either.

It probably had something to do with the slices of apples Nancy the receptionist always kept on hand for her.

"Do you still want to come inside for a few moments?"

"Of course. I didn't want to stay at your house any longer, but I am not quite ready to spend the rest of my day off by myself."

Thinking about Lorene's problems with her lost love, and how her grandmother had ruined her happiness, Viola felt so sorry for her.

She, too, was starting to know what it felt like to fall for the wrong man. So far, the only man she'd felt any spark for was Ed, and he was going to be leaving soon.

What if she never met anyone else who struck her fancy? Was a future like Lorene's in store? Was she destined to get a small house by herself because she was being too choosy?

Her thoughts shamed her. If she never married, it meant she could always be there for Elsie. Certainly, there would be no greater gift than the opportunity to always be there for her twin?

She was still thinking about that when they greeted the receptionist, said that Star probably wouldn't mind having a few apple slices, and then made her way to see Atle.

"This is a nice place," Lorene murmured.

"I forgot, you haven't been here before, have you?"

"Nope." Lorene looked at everyone curiously, smiling at a few of the ladies. But then her face froze when they entered the card room.

"What is it?"

"John is here."

It took a moment for Viola to figure out who Lorene was speaking of, but then it clicked. "*Your* John?"

"Jah." She stood awkwardly, looking like she might run away at any moment. But it was too late to go anywhere.

Both John and Ed were staring at them. Only Mr. Swartz was motioning them forward. He had a smile on his face, just as if they had shown up late for a party.

"Viola! You came, after all."

"I'm right on time," she said crisply. She paused, feeling the tension between John and Lorene as fiercely as if she were the one with the many regrets. Clearing her throat, she began the introductions. "Mr. Swartz, Edward, this is my aunt Lorene. Lorene, please meet Edward Swartz; his father, Atle, and . . ."

"This is my old friend John Miller," Ed finished with a slight look of amusement. "But I do believe that John and Lorene already know each other."

"We certainly know each other, don't we, Lorene?" John said. Even Viola heard the trace of sarcasm in his voice.

"We do." Lorene stared at him for a long moment before shaking her head, clearing out the cobwebs. "Please forgive my manners. It's nice to meet you, Mr. Swartz. And nice to see you again, Ed."

The other men added their greetings, and Ed said something, but Viola missed what he said. She couldn't help but watch Lorene and John. They kept staring at each other like the other one would disappear if they blinked.

Then John stepped forward. "Lorene, I need to apologize to you for the way I acted last week. My only excuse was that I was caught off guard, seeing you out of the blue like that."

"I can understand that," Lorene said. After a moment, she smiled at him.

And he smiled back.

And that's when Viola realized that her grandmother had been wrong when she'd gotten involved with Lorene's love life. She'd been foolish to try to stop what was there in front of all of them. No matter how much she had wanted to keep John and Lorene from each other, one thing was certain. Even after being apart for a decade, they'd managed to keep a connection.

John was still as perceptive as ever. That had been the first thing that Lorene had noticed about him—that he seemed to sense things deeply.

So much so, she'd soon realized she could never lie to him. Not even about the most inconsequential thing. If she said she wasn't cold when she was, he'd still find a blanket to put around her shoulders. If she said she wasn't bothered or upset about something, he had always shaken his head a bit sorrowfully. "Come now, Lorene," he'd say. "Don'tcha think it's time you were honest with me?"

Then, before she'd realize what was happening, she would be telling him what was really wrong, even if it had something to do with him. His kindness and openness had been a revelation. In her family, appearance and orderliness had been valued above personal happiness. Until John, she hadn't realized that it was possible to be completely open with anyone.

But things between them hadn't lasted long. When her mother had found out about John's intentions, she'd been horrified, and had quickly and brutally pointed out every one of his flaws. And his family's flaws.

And then compared his weaknesses to their family's strengths. From every angle, a relationship with John had seemed full of folly. Like the worst sort of romance.

And so she'd broken things off, and had been completely honest and open with him, just in the way John had taught her. She'd told him how she felt, and what she was sure was wrong with him. She'd been careful to not leave out a single problem. Before her eyes, he'd distanced himself from her.

Told her to leave.

Only weeks later did she realize that while she'd been honest with him about her feelings, she'd been wrong. All the things that had seemed so very important at the time hadn't mattered in the long run.

Now, here she was, struggling with the same feelings that she'd had all those years ago.

"I should go," she blurted.

Viola blinked. "Right now?"

"*Jah*. It's better if I leave, I think."

"May I walk you home?" John asked.

It was time to clear the air, even if it made her feel even worse than before. "Sure."

He smiled, joined her in saying goodbye to everyone, then stood at the door, waiting for her to follow.

When they were outside, he paused. "Which way?"

"Right. I live only six blocks away."

"When did you move out this way?"

"About four years ago."

"Any special reason?"

There were many reasons, some too private to share. "It was time." But in an effort to regain some of her honesty, she added, "I started to realize that I might never get married. I was tired of waiting for the perfect time to have my own home."

"I can't believe we haven't run into each other."

"John, I'm surprised at you. Now you're the one who's lying." She was sure they'd both taken pains to avoid each other.

After a moment's hesitation, he spoke. "I learned that being completely honest doesn't do a man many favors." The muscles in his throat worked. "At times, it's better to keep some things to oneself."

Lorene knew his comment was a jab at their past. No matter how she'd tried to tell him that she'd broken up with him in order to honor her parents, he'd been sure she'd rejected him because of his lack of money and social standing. "That is true, but it's also true that sometimes truthfulness isn't believed." They stopped at a light, waited for the traffic to pass before crossing the street. "Just three more blocks."

"Is that what happened, Lorene?" he murmured. "You told me the truth, but I didn't believe it?"

"That is some of it." Even now, she couldn't put all the blame on his shoulders.

"Then what did happen?"

She thought about her mother chiding her about John. About her father insisting that she wait for a better, more worthy man. Thought about how unsure she'd begun to feel about herself, how she'd started second-guessing every decision she made. "Everything."

"What is that supposed to mean?"

There was no way she'd ever be able to explain herself in only a few words. "I'd rather talk about it when we have more time." She half winced. Ready for him to push her again, like he used to do.

But he remained silent.

They picked up their pace. Crossed another intersection, then, at least, her house was in sight. "It's just up there. On the right."

It was a small home, built years ago, in

the forties. The owner had made it into duplexes and rented them out. From the moment she'd moved in, it had felt like the right place for her. Her neighbor was a woman about her age. Mennonite. Every once in a while, they'd share a cup of coffee or a couple of cookies or dinner together. And just down the street lived Sam and Mary Beth and their three Ds.

"This is nice," he said.

"It's been nice for me."

"Lorene, ever since you stopped by the store, I've hardly been able to think of anything but you. Do you really think it's possible for us to start over?"

"Yes. At least, I do."

Relief filled his eyes, echoing the way she felt. "I'd like to see you again."

"I'd like that, too."

"May I stop by to see you sometime soon?"

"Of course." She wondered when that would be.

He nodded, then turned away. Without another word.

But of course, there really wasn't anything else either of them needed to say.

What mattered now were actions. He needed to see that she was willing to commit to him, not be caged by her parents' narrow-mindedness. She was her own woman now and she finally knew what she wanted—John Miller in her life again.

chapter fourteen

Viola, Ed, and his father were still talking about Lorene and John leaving together the way they did, even though they'd left a half hour ago.

"I don't know either of them, but it looks like love to me," his father quipped. "Once they saw each other, no one else seemed to exist."

"Daed, I never knew you could sound so romantic."

"Oh, I've had romance in my life. Your mother and I were married over thirty years."

Ed shared a smile with Viola. "I guess he does know a thing or two about romance."

"Much more than I," Viola concurred. "I've never seen my aunt act like that. Usually she's terribly reserved around men."

"That young man looked like he couldn't wait to be alone with her."

Once again, Viola found she was charmed by Atle's frankness. "I thought the same thing," she said hesitantly. "Ed, is your friend John usually so direct?"

"I didn't think so, but I haven't seen him in a few years." He shrugged.

"I hope they will be okay. People can change, you know."

Mr. Swartz chuckled softly. "Don't you worry about those two, Viola. I have a feeling that everything that's happening between them is happening for a reason. God has decided it was the right time for them to chat."

Ed raised his brows. "Daed, you decided all of that after observing them only for just a few minutes?"

"Son, you were only fifteen back then, and far more interested in your problems than anyone else's. But I vividly remember that man fretting something awful when the two of them broke things off. He was as brokenhearted as I've ever seen."

"I guess I was unaware of their drama," Edward mused. "Ten years ago, I had just finished school and was trying to figure out what I wanted to do with my life."

"Ten years ago, you were concerned with far more than just work," his *daed* said with a chuckle. "I seem to remember you far more interested in running around." He stretched his hands, grimacing as if his joints were paining him. "But as for John, well, he grew up in a sad house. There was a lot of pain there. Though he never said much, I have a feeling that there were forces involved that were out of his control."

"I know what you're speaking of," Viola said. "My, uh, grandmother didn't favor their relationship."

"It wasn't just Lorene's family that had put up obstacles. His father wasn't completely ready for John to fall in love and get married, either." After a pause, he added, "I happen to think the Lord has plans for all of us, all in His own time, too. Perhaps one day your aunt and John Miller will understand why they needed to stay apart for a while."

Ed nodded. "I hear what you're saying, but sometimes it's hard to always follow

His will." Looking at Viola, he shrugged. "Even as a missionary, I still wonder about the Lord's plans for us all. Every once in a while, I see things that make me question His will."

Privately, Viola had wondered about that quite a bit. She'd never understood why she had been blessed with perfect health while her twin had been given an eye disease.

"God don't offer us an easy life, Edward," his father said. "Just a good one. For some reason, you are being called to serve far away from home. You've thrived, and I've accepted that."

"But don't you miss each other?" The moment Viola asked the question, she ached to take it back.

Mr. Swartz looked at her in surprise. "But of course I miss him. He's my only child. But just because something hurts, it don't mean that it shouldn't happen." Folding his hands primly on his lap, he eyed her over the tops of his wire-rimmed glasses. "Jesus himself taught us that, Girly."

She had no idea what to say to that. But she knew there was truth in the old man's statement.

"You always make me mighty glad I work here, Mr. Swartz. You've given me a lot to think about today."

"We don't have to think so much, you know," Ed said quietly. "Not all the time, at least."

"What do you mean?"

He pushed a Scrabble game toward her. "Do you have time for a quick game? How about all we think about is scoring points?"

"I think that is a fine idea." Pleased that all of the big issues were being pushed aside for the time being, Viola picked up a pen. "I'll be scorekeeper."

Atle rolled his eyes. "You're always scorekeeper."

"I'm better at it than you." She waited a beat, and winked at Ed. "Besides, you always cheat."

"Modesty ain't your strong point, Viola. Your willful tongue ain't, either."

"I know, sir. I'm working on it. It's a gift I hope God will explain to me one day." When she cast a glance in Ed's direction, she saw that he smiled.

Well, they'd survived yet another church hosting. When Lovina was younger, she'd bounced back from all the work a little bit easier.

Now? Even on Monday she was already ready for a nap.

Lovina lay down on the neatly made bed and closed her eyes. She knew every Amish family felt the same pressure she did to present their house in the best possible way.

But sometimes she felt as if the stress of the preparations far outweighed the benefits of communing together in each other's homes.

She heard the door open. "Lovina, are you asleep?" Aaron asked.

She remained still with her eyes closed. She probably wasn't fooling him for a second, but she didn't want to talk. All she wanted to do was lie down and remember other times. Some memories were happy. Others?

Not so much.

Such as when she and Aaron had hosted church for the very first time.

She'd only recently joined the church, though she and Aaron had been married for over a year. But she'd viewed hosting church as a milestone in their life together.

After all, it was the first time that many in their community would see them together as a couple. It was also the first time she had hosted such a large number of people. She'd had nightmares of running out of food.

As she'd expected, the day of the service she was a nervous wreck. She'd been baking cookies since sunrise, and every other batch seemed either burned or too doughy. Or the wrong size.

Looking back, Lovina realized she'd been striving for perfection when none was needed. No one needed perfect cookies, just as others would have helped with the baking, if only she'd been confident enough to admit that she couldn't do it all.

But she'd been the exact opposite of confident. She'd been so insecure in her abilities that every wrongdoing had seemed magnified. Sure that every flaw would make Aaron realize that he'd made a terribly wrong decision when he'd asked her to marry him.

She'd ended up putting only three dozen cookies on the tray. And she'd had trouble with the other dishes, too. Her egg salad was too mustardy, causing her to throw out a whole batch. Her relish didn't taste fresh enough. She'd overcooked the noo-dles for the macaroni salad.

After the service, everyone lined up to get the food . . . and, indeed, they'd run out.

"Lovina, where's the rest of it?" Aaron had asked, his voice holding a thick note of worry.

"This is everything."

"Are you sure?"

"Of course." Stung by his look of dismay, her tone had turned defensive. Clipped.

He scratched his beard. "But we bought enough. I know we did, I asked the Bren-namens how much they made of every-thing and wrote it down for you."

"This wasn't your fault, Aaron."

He motioned to the rather small bowl of macaroni salad. "I thought I bought three boxes of pasta. I'm no cook, but I know three boxes make more than this. Did you make it all?"

She couldn't do it any longer. "I made it," she said, her voice catching. "I made it all, but not everything was good enough," she said. "So I threw it out." Now tears filled her eyes.

Immediately, his confused expression turned to worry. "Lovina, what are we going to do?"

"I don't know," she'd said simply.

But what she'd wished more than anything was for him to wrap an arm around her shoulders and pull her close to him for a hug.

She'd yearned for him to talk to her, right then and there. Tell her that she did everything just fine. That everyone made mistakes.

To tell her that she didn't need to be a perfect Amish wife, that all she needed to be was herself.

She raised her eyes and stared into his. Waited for him to do something, anything to show her that he loved her.

He opened his mouth. Looked like he was about to tell her everything she wanted. But then he turned around and walked away.

In front of the other ladies.

They'd looked at her with pity.

She'd been too insecure to realize that if she'd only smiled their way and asked them for help, they would have surrounded her with all their industry. That they would have run to her kitchen and whipped up something easily.

But because she hadn't reached out, they'd stayed where they were, warily watching her.

So she did the only thing she could. And that was to hold her head up and pretend that she wasn't upset.

If there was one thing she was good at, it was pretending that her heart never burned and her feelings never got hurt.

Hmm. It seemed that she had perfected something after all.

chapter fifteen

It was snowing heavily when Ed arrived at the Christian Aid Ministry Association office at nine A.M. the next morning.

"Thanks for picking me up, Jared," he said when they got out of the man's rather spiffy black SUV.

"It was no problem. It would've been a difficult walk in the snow." He looked to say more, but his cell phone buzzed.

With a small wave, Ed walked on, giving the other man his privacy, and allowing him a few precious seconds to get his bearings.

The rather plain, nondescript building

always made him smile when he approached it. The CAMA headquarters didn't look special or especially grand. Inside, however, it was filled with people who made huge differences around the whole world.

Shivering a bit under the thin comfort of his wool coat, Ed was thankful for the blast of heat that greeted him. Once again, it struck him how different he was after just twenty-four months in Nicaragua. The coat he was wearing had long been a favorite. He'd had it for years, and it had kept him warm and comfortable through many a difficult winter.

Now, however, the coat's fabric felt little better than a sheet of cotton, and he felt the chill all the way deep into his bones. Not wanting Jared to have to wait for him, he'd stood on his front porch for ten minutes before he arrived. Now his body felt like it was regretting every minute of it.

Was he getting soft? Or perhaps, he was simply getting old enough to appreciate being warm and dry instead of chilled and damp? Maybe he shouldn't blame his *daed* for not wanting to leave the comforts of Daybreak.

He pondered these big questions while

he wandered around the lobby of the Mission offices, waiting for the chairman, James Cross, to finish up a phone call and invite him into his office.

The waiting wasn't anything new. Mr. Cross was a busy man, and a good one. Like many others in the organization, he seemed to constantly be running five minutes late—the consequences of trying to do too much in too little time.

Usually, he never minded the delay. Usually, he would let the receptionist know he'd arrived, then have a seat for a bit until someone had time to meet with him. But the summons to the offices felt important. He couldn't put a finger on why he felt that way, but he had the strangest feeling that his life was about to change.

After two more minutes, Mr. Cross entered the lobby. "Good morning, Edward. I'd apologize for keeping you waiting, but Patricia here has reminded me time and again that my tardiness has become something of a habit."

"I didn't mind." He rubbed his arms a bit comically. "It gave me time to get warmed up. It seems I've gotten used to the warmer temperatures of Central America."

Mr. Cross chuckled. He held out his hands. "Let me take your coat and hat for you. And coffee? Would you like some hot coffee?"

Feeling somewhat awkward, Ed handed over his coat and hat to the head of the organization. "*Danke*. And, um, *jah, kaffi* sounds *wunderbaar*."

Mr. Cross hung up his things in a closet Edward had never noticed before. "Good, we'll get you a cup right away." He patted him on the back. "And thanks again for agreeing to meet with us today. I know it was short notice."

Ed shrugged. He worked for the organization. It was his duty to come when he was asked to. And a week's notice didn't seem too short to him. "Um, it was no problem, Mr. Cross."

"James," he corrected.

"James," he repeated awkwardly. "And, uh, as you know, I live nearby." Of course he would meet him at a moment's notice!

"Yes, it is our luck that you live right here in Berlin. Since you've been back you've been spending time with your father, right?" he asked over his shoulder as he led the way down a narrow carpeted hall to his office.

"Yes, I have," he replied, though he was starting to realize that he hadn't come to Berlin just to pay his father a visit. No, instead, it was to reclaim his past and make peace with it.

"And how is he doing?"

"He is in good health," Ed said slowly, enjoying the feeling of warmth that was slowly easing into his muscles. As they continued down the hall, the walls decorated with neatly framed photographs of missionaries in different parts of the world, he added, "My father seems to enjoy living at Daybreak very much."

"Ah, yes. That's the retirement home on Market Street, isn't it?"

"That's the one."

"It seems like a nice facility. Big."

Thinking of the many rooms that he always had to go through in order to locate his father, Ed nodded. "It is that. There's always a lot going on there, too. Speakers and such." Continuing awkwardly, he said, "I listened to a wildlife lecture with him last week."

Pausing at the doorway, Mr. Cross said, "I'm very glad you told me that he's happy there. It makes me feel even better about calling you like I did."

Edward followed him into his office, then stopped abruptly when he realized they weren't going to be meeting alone. At a small circular table sat three other people with folders and notebooks in front of them.

All three stopped talking and looked at him.

Feeling vaguely on display, he lifted a hand in an awkward greeting.

The chairman walked to his side and rested a palm on one of his shoulder blades. "Everyone, you remember Edward Swartz. Ed, this is Grace Adams and Michele Evans. And Jared Schilling, of course."

Once introductions were over, Mr. Cross pointed to the sole empty chair. "Take a seat, Edward."

Ed sat, but when he eyed the pens in everyone else's hands, he knew he had to speak up. Looking around the circular oak table, his impatience got the worst of him. "Forgive me for being so blunt, but what, exactly, is this meeting about? I had assumed it was going to be an update on my experience in Nicaragua."

James and Jared shook their heads.

"No, we didn't ask you to come here to discuss Nicaragua, Ed," Mr. Cross said. Taking a deep breath, he continued, "Actually, we called you here to offer you a new position."

"A new position?"

"Indeed." With a wide smile, he said, "Edward, we want you to become the director of our Belize mission."

"I didn't know we had a mission in Belize."

"We don't. Yet," Michele said.

"The person we had in mind to launch the program is fighting off some health difficulties, I'm afraid. You were our next logical choice."

"Me?" Ed felt himself stare blankly at Mr. Cross.

"We think you'll do very well there, Ed."

Though he knew he sounded foolish, he made himself clarify what he was hearing. "You want me to be a director? A director of the Belize mission."

Mr. Cross nodded, as if everything was

getting all cleared up. "That's right. We've had to do quite a bit of personnel shifting due to the recent downturn in the economy. The donations simply aren't coming in like they used to, which means we can't staff each missionary site the way we'd like."

"Our first priority is for the people we serve," Michele said.

"Yes, that makes sense," Ed agreed. Everything made sense, except for his part in the staffing.

"So, we decided to talk to you about heading up the Belize mission. You'd be starting from scratch. We have a building for you, and a team of five from the office ready to accompany you there, and help you understand the extent of your responsibilities."

"It's an exciting opportunity," Jared said with an easy smile. "Not many people are offered the opportunity to do this. You would be able to set up the mission how you think it would work best, and you'd get to handpick the locals on staff."

But he didn't feel ready. "I've only done one two-year stint."

Mr. Cross smiled. "I realize that, but you showed an immense amount of maturity and leadership skills. Everyone was impressed with you, Edward. A lot of people feel called to work in this field, but sometimes God doesn't always gift them with the skills to do the real work that needs to be done. In your case, however, it seems as if the Lord created you specifically for mission work. You have a natural affinity for it."

The chairman's words were terribly kind. Ed appreciated hearing the words of praise, and it was nice that others had noticed his hard work.

But he didn't feel ready.

Perhaps it was the devil bringing his fears to light? His mother had always told him that God's timing was impeccable. Even when he wasn't sure, the Lord knew what he was doing. Faith was believing in the Lord enough to follow His lead.

"Could you tell me more about this position, and the job as well?" he asked. "When would you want me to go? How many times would I go down before living there permanently?"

For the first time, everyone assembled looked uneasy.

Which, of course, made him shift in his seat.

"We would want you to get started on this mission as soon as possible," Grace said. She tapped an open calendar with the eraser end of a bright blue pencil.

Ed noticed she was tapping a January calendar page. Warily, he said, "I was scheduled to be on leave for six months. That will end in June. So, you are planning for me to begin at the start of summer?"

Looking at little uneasy, Grace shook her head. "We don't want to wait that long. We were hoping to have you go out there next week."

So the open calendar wasn't a mistake. Ed felt like a vise was steadily tightening around his chest. And though he hated to admit his hesitation, he didn't think he should be anything but honest. "I don't know if I'm prepared to do that."

"I know this is sudden, but you would only stay there for two weeks," Mr. Cross said. "Plus I have to say with all this snow we're having, the chance to be in Belize for two weeks right now doesn't sound like a hardship."

No, it sounded like an eternity. "And then?"

Grace smiled reassuringly. "While there,

you would make note of what supplies you would need, continue the staffing process, talk with the local clergy . . ." She shrugged. "It's a lot, of course, but I'm sure you would do fine."

He appreciated her belief in him, but she still hadn't answered his question about the next steps. "But if you are already wanting to hire people, it sounds as if you are planning to open this mission right away."

Mr. Cross nodded. "That's right. We would want you to return to Belize full-time by mid-February."

There it was. They were expecting him to have barely two weeks off after working solidly for two years. Then set up a new office and mission, which would be far more work and responsibility than he was used to. "And stay for how long? Two years?"

"Well, actually, five," Grace said. "We wouldn't want to put someone into place, just to move them right away. It takes time to gain trust in the community. And it takes time for you to see the differences you're making in other people's lives."

Five years.

In five years he'd be thirty. He'd always imagined that he'd be married with a child or two by the time he reached thirty years old. But if he was in Belize?

Marriage and children would have to be pushed off to the future. "I don't know. . . ."

Michele curved her hands around her coffee cup. "I know you're taken aback. You have every right to be; what we're asking is neither easy to do, nor easy to plan for."

Mr. Cross spoke again. "Edward, we've looked at the list of candidates, and we all feel you're the best fit for this job. Yes, there are other people in the organization with more experience, but we don't feel that any of them would be the best person to open up a mission. You're it, Ed. We've all prayed about this, and we all are in accordance, you would be a wonderful director for Belize."

"Of course, you should pray about this, too," Grace added. "No one expects you to give an answer right now."

But he had a feeling that wasn't quite true. The decision had been made and they were merely waiting for him to climb on board and get with the program. "There are a great many things to consider," he said slowly. "My father, for one—"

"I know you'll miss him, but you said

yourself that he's happy where he is," Mr. Cross smoothly interrupted. "Plus, I'm sure he will be mighty proud of you. Your work will make a great many people's lives better. And, of course, the mission is greatly needed. There's something to be said for that."

In theory, Ed agreed with all that they were saying. Perhaps if he was still in Nicaragua, he'd be less apprehensive.

But he was home in Ohio now, and even during this short time, he'd been reminded of all he'd given up in order to do his mission work. "I need time to think about your offer. I just opened up our house again. . . ." What he didn't dare mention was that at the moment, his father and the house were only some of what he was thinking about. If he left, he'd be leaving so much behind. Gretta, and his new friendship with John . . . and Viola!

Viola most of all, he realized. Here, he'd been practically courting her. Taking her to lunch, taking her out for pie. Attending church services at her house.

What was he supposed to do? Simply ignore his feelings for her?

As that shock ran through his body, Mr.

Cross pushed a pair of thick binders toward him from across the table. "Edward, please don't be worried. We know we've given you a lot to think about. Take these binders and read through them. Talk to your father and your friends. Pray on it. Then give us a call."

That was good advice. Feeling like he was finally given a moment to process it all, he stood up and hugged the binders to his chest. He could do this. He could pray and read and gather the courage to tell his father that he might be leaving him far sooner than they'd anticipated. "When do you need to know if I will take the assignment?"

"We'll need to know within the next three days if you don't want to go," Jared said.

"I see."

Everyone else stood up, too. "Ed, do you think you'll be able to do that?" the chairman asked.

"Yes, sir. I will." It wasn't like he had a choice about it. Needing some time to himself, he turned to Jared. "I think I'm going to go ahead and walk home."

"Are you sure? It's snowing pretty hard out."

"I'm sure. I've got my boots on."

"Thanks for coming in, Edward," Mr. Cross said warmly.He shook Ed's hand, then turned back to the others in the room.

Ed was happy to be on his way. After grabbing his coat and hat from the closet, he exited and was met with a face full of snow. By nightfall, the roads would barely be passable. It looked as if the Lord was giving him the opportunity to sit and read and pray and reflect in peace and quiet.

As he tucked his chin and starting walking briskly home, he started praying for God to give him some guidance and strength.

This was such a big decision, he knew he was going to need all the help he could get.

chapter sixteen

It had been snowing for almost twelve hours straight, and when Viola woke up and saw how thick the covering was, she knew there was no way she was going to be able to leave the house.

A thick feeling of disappointment settled deep in her chest as she realized that she couldn't go into work.

Which meant, of course, that she wasn't going to be able to see Ed. Thinking about Monday, when they'd gone out for pie and talked so much that she'd practically forgotten to eat, she sighed. Something unexpected and wonderful was happening to their relationship. He was making her see the world in a brand-new way, and also examine her own faith. Suddenly, she was more aware of Jesus's presence in her life, and that awareness felt like a wonderful gift.

Pushing her disappointment away, she went to the kitchen where their phone was, called Daybreak, and explained the situation to Mrs. Ames.

Luckily, Mrs. Ames completely understood and told Viola that she'd call her early Thursday morning to let her know how the roads were.

After the phone call was done, Viola slipped on a rather subdued and old gray dress. It was by far her least favorite dress. She'd mismeasured when she'd cut the fabric, and it always felt a bit too tight in the shoulders and too loose around her hips and waist. But it was perfect for cleaning and it suited her mood.

When Elsie saw her in her old gray dress, she grinned. "You aiming to make sure we all know you're unhappy, Viola?"

Elsie was always able to practically read her mind.

Not that she needed to know that, of

course. "I simply didn't want to get a newer dress dirty."

"That's a *gut* excuse if I ever heard one."

Viola glanced at her twin sharply. She was almost positive that Elsie was being sarcastic. Almost. But instead of calling her out, she let it slide. She supposed she was wearing her heart on her sleeve.

"I'm simply disappointed not to be working, that's all."

"And, perhaps, not seeing Edward Swartz?"

"That does have something to do with it," she said with a sheepish smile. After taking care to make sure no one else was in hearing distance, Viola softened her resolve to keep her feelings close to her heart. "Elsie, I don't know what's happened to me, but I can't seem to stop thinking about him!"

"He is handsome."

Viola's heart beat a little faster. "He is."

"And he doesn't let you walk over him, either. That's in his favor."

"I'm not that bossy."

"You're pretty bossy, sister, with most everyone."

"Except for Edward." But of course, this wasn't exactly true. She'd tried to tell him what to do, just like she did with everyone else, but he ignored her completely. This should have made her peeved. Instead, it made her respect him all the more.

"Well, that means something, I think." Smiling whimsically, Elsie said, "Maybe you are ready to admit you're falling in love."

"I hope not. He's not the right one for me."

"God might think differently."

"God might, but even He knows that falling in love with Ed would be a big mistake." Though, was it? she wondered. Whenever she thought of him, she wanted to smile. And now that she knew there was no chance of seeing him? She felt a little sick. Those were all the signs, weren't they?

"I don't know if it would be a mistake, Viola. From what I can tell, Edward is a good man." Somewhat dryly Elsie added, "They're not all like that, you know."

"Believe me, I know."

"Plus, he's easy on the eyes. A nice bonus, I think."

"I didn't think you could see him all that well," she blurted before she stopped herself. "Oh my goodness, Elsie. Please forgive me. I didn't mean it like it sounded."

Quick tears sprang to Elsie's eyes, but she blinked them away as if they didn't matter in the slightest. "There's nothing to forgive, Viola. Though what I did see I found terribly handsome. You are exactly right—I don't see well." Lowering her voice, she confided, "Sometimes it feels like I'm losing my sight a little more each day."

The pain and guilt she always felt whenever they talked about Elsie's eyesight returned like an old enemy. "I didn't know your sight was diminishing so quickly," she said, remembering the many struggles Elsie had encountered over the years. First in school, when they'd discovered she needed glasses, then the moment in the doctor's office when he'd shared the awful truth about her disease. "H-Have you told Mamm?" she stuttered, ashamed again at her inability to speak of her twin's disease in a more detached way.

"Of course not," Elsie said lightly.

"You should."

"Viola, you know why I haven't. Mamm would only rush me to the doctor."

"Elsie, that would be because you need to go!" What she didn't add but ached to was that they needed to ask more questions, check into more options. Maybe even take a bus to the famous Cleveland Clinic instead of relying on local doctors. Someone had to help her. Late at night, when she allowed her fears to get the best of her, Viola worried that their chosen way of life had interfered with the best possible medical care for her sister. Perhaps if they'd had greater access to other folks, or to more magazines or to television shows, her parents would have fought Elsie's deteriorating condition more aggressively.

But this was not a feeling Elsie shared. "I have a feeling that it won't matter how many doctors I go to. None of them are going to be able to tell me anything new."

"You don't know that for sure."

"But I do, sister," Elsie said gently. Almost as if she was worrying about hurting Viola with her news. "See, years ago, Dr. Kopple told me that I was going blind. I've come to terms with that."

"I haven't."

"That's because you are used to pecking at everyone like a hen, forcing everyone to listen to you. You, dear twin, are a woman who likes getting her way."

"You make me sound pretty selfish."

"Not selfish, just headstrong," Elsie corrected. "And I don't think that there's anything wrong with that. All of us need someone in our lives like you. Having someone question and prod and push can be a blessing." She shrugged. "However, in this instance it wouldn't do any good."

Feeling embarrassed, Viola knew it was time to change topics. "I don't have to clean. Instead, I could start piecing you a new dress?"

"*Nee.* Mommi is doing that for me today. And I know Mamm wants the insides of some of the cabinets to be cleaned out and organized today."

"In the kitchen?" Viola said hopefully.

"No, in the hall and bathrooms."

Viola wrinkled her nose. She hated cleaning out bathroom cabinets. She didn't like contorting herself on the bathroom floor in order to change the liners on the bottom of the cabinets. "I'm glad I wore my gray dress. It's going to be a long day."

Elsie chuckled. "It could be worse. Mamm asked if I'd rather pluck chickens in the barn."

"I hate that even more."

"Me, too," Elsie said with a small smile

as she started walking down the hall. "I told Mamm that Roman can do that chore."

"He hates plucking chickens even more than we do!"

"I know, but I told Mamm that with my eyes, cleaning out cabinets would be much better for me," she said with a knowing smile.

For the first time that morning, Viola laughed.

Though it was barely two o'clock, Peter felt as if it had already been the longest day he'd had in weeks. It was the snow's doing, of course. If it hadn't been snowing, he would have taken care of the horses, then hitched up the buggy and gone into town. He'd had a meeting scheduled with the banker.

But that of course had to be canceled. So, he'd put on his warmest coat, grabbed his gloves and snow shovel, and then gotten busy.

The fresh blanket of snow meant more chores than usual for him and Roman. Paths to the main house, barn, and *dawdi house* needed to be shoveled. Animals needed to be checked on and moved inside the barn. After he'd wrung the necks of two hens, he'd left Roman with the ugly task of plucking them while he went inside for a bit of hot coffee.

When he walked into the kitchen, he found Marie on her hands and knees, a fierce expression on her face.

"Marie, what in the world is going on?"

She rocked back on her heels. "Oh, Peter, I'm so glad to see you! We have a mouse."

Marie could take care of just about anything, except mice. She was by turns scared of them and the fiercest of hunters. One squeak could send her squealing like a teenage girl. She'd never failed to amuse him with her squeamishness around them, either. "Marie, you should've come to get me. I would've taken care of it for you."

His comment didn't appease her in the slightest. "If I'd gotten up to find you, I would've lost sight of the mouse." Leaning down again, she frowned. "Though I'm afraid this one got away. Peter, we need to put out more traps."

"All right," he soothed.

"The sooner the better, too. This one gave me a fright when I opened the cabinet."

There was only one thing to do, of course. Help her locate it. "Let me get a flashlight, then I'll help you mouse hunt."

"*Danke,* Peter."

She looked so relieved, he smiled to himself. Even after all this time, when she looked at him that way, her eyes wide and languid, she made him feel like he was ten feet tall.

Kneeling beside her, he shone the light into the cupboard. Pulled out a container of sugar, and a carton of salt. And was just about to pull out another carton when a shrill squeak erupted, barely a half a second before the interloper appeared. It squeaked again. Loudly.

Startled, he jumped. Beside him, Marie gave a cry of dismay.

And then another mouse appeared, and he had nothing more than a silver flashlight in his hands. What to do?

"Two!" Marie exclaimed. "Oh, but this is terrible!" she squealed when both mice started scurrying to them. Jumping to his feet, he grabbed her rolling pin, leaned back down, did a twist, then slammed it down hard onto the bottom of the cabinet.

A tiny puff of flour appeared.

Amazingly, he killed both in that one fatal blow.

Still holding the rolling pin, he looked at his wife proudly. "Marie, your mouse problem is solved."

"But you ruined my rolling pin in the process!"

He laughed. "It can be washed, dear. Now, hand me some paper towels and I'll dispose of the bodies."

After another moment of staring at the pin in shock, she started giggling. And then her giggles turned to bright laughter. Making the dreary, snowy day seem like the best day in years.

He set the tainted rolling pin down on the ground and held her in his arms as she continued to laugh.

"Oh, Peter! I can't believe you clubbed the mice!"

"I couldn't help myself. And I'm right proud of myself, too! I still have good reflexes."

"Indeed! We could hire you out, you and my rolling pin!"

He started laughing, too, finally sitting on the floor next to Marie and wrapping an arm around her. "I haven't laughed so much in ages."

She wiped her eyes. "Me, either."

"I think you need a kitten, though. A good mouser."

Sweet hope entered her eyes."You'd get me a kitten?"

"Of course, Marie. I'll ask around in town. We'll find you a kitten."

"It would be fun, to have a little kitten for a bit, don't you think? The kids are so old . . ."

"Ah, Marie. You need something little to cuddle, don't you?"

"Maybe." Her gaze soft, she smiled into his eyes. Looking at him with so much love that his heart felt lighter than it had in months.

All at once, he was reminded of when they were courting. He'd used to take her driving in his courting buggy. And when the streets were empty, they'd *clip clop* along quietly, and he'd hold her hand.

And think about kissing her. After weeks went by, he did, indeed, kiss her. Sweet, chaste kisses, promising a lifetime of so much more. It had all been so special.

Looking at her now, seeing the love shining in her eyes, he leaned closer, tempted by the promise of her smile. By the sweet memories when their lives weren't so full of responsibilities.

As if she'd read his mind, Marie blinked, then lifted her head, offering him her lips, right there on the kitchen floor. Just as if they both weren't fortysomething, with three grown children.

For a moment, they were only Marie and Peter, and he still thought he was the luckiest man in the world to have her.

He kissed her lightly. Kissed her again. Smiled to himself when her hand reached around his neck and pulled him closer.

"Mamm? Daed? Oh, my gosh, what are you two doing?" Viola's voice called out, her voice hard.

They broke apart. For a moment Peter was tempted to say that it was fairly obvious . . . but then something in her tone caught his attention. With effort, he climbed to his feet. "What is it, daughter?"

She strode forward, her expression pinched. "Elsie and I need to show you something."

Marie stood up and brushed out her dress. "Is it a mouse, dear?"

"Not a mouse. It is something much worse."

He shared a look with Marie. "What did you find?"

"Elsie and I found a bottle of vodka. Under the sink in the bathroom."

As the words sank in, he felt his world spin a bit. He'd been so captivated by Marie, he'd completely forgotten about that stashed bottle.

How could he have been so foolhardy?

Beside him, Marie's body turned to stone. And he knew at that moment that it was going to be a very long time before they'd be kissing again.

Before she'd look at him with such love again.

Yes, just like that, the mood was broken. There was also a very good chance that he might never get it back.

chapter seventeen

Himler's Cheese Shop was practically a Berlin landmark. It had been around for generations, though only in the Alpine-looking building for thirty or forty years. Some were tempted to proclaim that the shop was merely a tourist attraction. And it was true, a great many tourists did choose to visit the store.

But it was more than that. Men and women made the cheese the same as they always had, in painstaking processes that created velvety Goudas and sharp cheddars. Locals stopped by often. And many more folks ordered various cheeses to be shipped across the country.

Lorene Keim had always enjoyed working there. She liked being a part of something bigger than herself, even if it was only a cheese shop in tiny Berlin, Ohio.

Even though the weather was snowy, she'd arrived at eight o'clock that morning. She'd enjoyed walking to the store in her thick boots over the snow-packed sidewalks. Hardly anyone had been on the roads, and the resulting silence, broken only by the shrill trill of a bright cardinal, had been music to her ears.

Soon after checking in with Frank, she'd gotten right to work. She helped fill a few orders, straightened the counters surrounding the checkout area, and counted the money for the opening balance of the cash register.

Then greeted and assisted the first arriving customers.

A tour bus from Cleveland hadn't let the heavy snow slow it down. It parked in the parking lot a full thirty minutes ahead of schedule. And when the bus doors opened, at least forty people piled out and trotted into the store.

Some took the tour of the cheese factory. Most, however, entertained themselves by sampling the many varieties of cheese the store had to offer and filling plastic grocery baskets. Two hours sped by as she rang up sales and answered questions, both about the cheese shop and being Amish.

When that group left, a few locals arrived, and kept them all busy enough so that the time didn't drag. So, it was a good day, with plenty to do . . . even if it wasn't anything out of the ordinary.

And then John came in.

She noticed other women—both Amish and English—pause in their conversations to take a first and second look at him. He truly was that handsome. If he noticed, he didn't give any indication of it. When a few folks stopped to say hello, he talked with them politely, but it was obvious to Lorene that he had come for only one reason, and that was to see her. Every few seconds he glanced her way.

She knew because she couldn't seem to tear her gaze away from him for more than a few seconds at a time. The other girls who worked with her noticed and giggled.

Lorene's hands trembled a bit as she counted change for an elderly man from Columbus. She told herself it was merely nerves; she wasn't used to being the center of attention. And everyone, it seemed, was looking at her and her visitor.

Looking up, she was shocked to see him staring right back at her. His gaze was steady, unwavering.

Which, of course, made her suddenly feel sixteen again.

"John. This is a surprise."

"It shouldn't be," he murmured. "I told you I wanted to see you again."

Goose bumps appeared on her arms. "Um . . . I know, but I didn't think you meant so soon," she blurted before giving the gentleman his receipt. "Thank you. Come again."

When the man walked away, Lorene prepared herself to ring up the next person's order. But no one was there—only John.

Quietly she mumbled, "John, I can't talk to you now."

Perfect white teeth flashed. "I know. I merely stopped by to ask if you'd like to come over for supper. I'm making beef and barley soup."

Supper. With John. At his house. Help-less anticipation coursed right through her.

Shaking it off, she asked, "You're cook-ing?"

"Don't sound so shocked," he chided. "I live on my own, Lorene. Just because I'm a man, it doesn't mean I can't cut up meat and vegetables and add some broth."

He was exactly right. And worse, she had a vague feeling that she was sound-ing a bit like her mother, who was the last person she wanted to sound like. "Supper sounds mighty nice. Especially since it's so snowy and cold out."

"*Gut*. What time do you get off?"

"Four o'clock."

"I'll be back then and walk you home, then to my *haus*."

The idea of his coming back for her, and everyone seeing that, made her cheeks heat like they were on fire. "You don't need to go to so much trouble."

"That's where you're wrong, Lorene. Good day."

Wordlessly, she raised her hand in a poor example of a wave. But she didn't think he saw it. He was already walking out of the store, with at least a dozen pairs of eyes watching his broad back.

Only when he was out of the building did she dare exhale.

Missy, one of her best girlfriends at the store, giggled. Frank, who'd been leaning against the back wall, watching unabashedly, coughed.

Lorene felt her lips curve up so high, she didn't know if she'd ever be able to stop smiling.

Not even when a lady suddenly appeared and plopped down a basket filled almost to the brim with cartons of cheese, crackers, and candies. "I'm ready, miss."

Lorene forced herself to concentrate on work. Not on the way John's eyes had looked greener than ever, thanks to his forest green shirt. "Were you waiting on me? I'm sorry. I'll ring you up as quickly as I can."

"Oh, don't fret, dear. I was in love once, too."

As her cheeks burned, and Missy giggled a little more loudly, Lorene dared to wonder if her time for love had finally come. After all this time.

*   *   *

Still holding the bottle of liquor, and fortified with Elsie by her side, Viola did her
best to overcome her shock. What was
happening to her family?

And what was happening to her parents? Never before had she seen them be
anything but cordial to each other. Now
she walked in on them kissing on the
kitchen floor?

And that was nothing compared to the
bottle of liquor she and Elsie had uncovered. It had to be their father's. More than
once, she, Roman, and Elsie had noticed
him behaving strangely. Roman had even
commented on it one night. They'd put it
off to his being tired, and especially stressed
because of Mommi's secrets.

But all the while, Viola had suspected
that something else was going on. Of
course, suspecting something and seeing
the evidence were two different things.

When both her mother and father merely
stared at her in silence, she felt her temper go flying. "Are either of you going to
tell me what this is all about?"

"I am not about to talk to you when

you're using that tone of voice. You will stop it now, Viola," her mother ordered.

Viola recognized her mother's tone of voice, too. She was most displeased. And, Viola suspected, not just with her. Viola also realized that she was causing her father a great deal of discomfort. But even as her father's skin turned ghostly pale, she pushed for answers. She was tired of constantly pretending that everything was all right.

"Daed? Is this bottle yours? Have you been drinking?"

"Girls," he replied, "you will put that bottle down now and leave us."

Automatically, Elsie backed away.

Viola, on the other hand, wasn't quite so ready to end the conversation. Goodness, but her father was acting just like her grandmother—keeping secrets! "But I want to—"

"But nothing," her mother countered. "You two should learn to stay out of things that are none of your business."

"Not our business? We were cleaning out bathroom cabinets. It's not our fault Daed picked such a poor hiding place."

Her father turned away. Whether it was in shame or anger, Viola didn't know. But she did know that she'd certainly just gone too far. She bit her lip to keep from saying another word.

Luckily, Elsie, ever the peacemaker, spoke. "Mamm, if Daed is drinking, it is our business. We are members of this family, too. And we live here."

"Leave us," Mamm repeated, a little more loudly. "This is not your concern."

Viola knew the right thing to do was to obey her parents. But she couldn't believe them. They were frustrated by her grandparents keeping secrets, yet here they were doing the same thing. Maybe all of these secrets coming to light had made her be more obstinate than usual.

Or maybe she was still coming to terms with the fact that for most of her life she'd been a little too full of herself, thinking she was part of a group of people who had much to be proud about. Whatever the reason, she placed the bottle on the countertop, and crossed her arms over her chest. "I know if we walk away you will never bring this up again. We'll simply push it under the rug. But we mustn't. If Daed is drinking, it's a big problem, and it's all of our concern."

"I agree," Elsie said. "I'm sure Roman would, too."

"As do I," their grandmother said from the shadows of the hall.

Her father visibly flinched. "Mamm, I didn't know you were here."

In a voice as cold as ice, she said, "You know, I had wondered a time or two what was wrong with you. You seemed sluggish. Now I understand. You've let alcohol in this godly house. Into your body. I am terribly ashamed of you, Peter. I don't know what I am going to tell your father."

Viola heard Elsie inhale sharply. Their grandmother's words seemed especially out of place, given that they all knew she'd been keeping some whoppers of secrets to herself.

But even more amazing was their father's reaction. Before their eyes, his cheeks flushed and he stood taller. His back became straight and strong. And the look he shot at his mother was as dark and angry as Viola had ever seen it.

"I no longer care if you are ashamed of me or not."

"You should. I am your mother."

"Indeed you are. But I am not a boy, and I have not been one for a very long time. There is nothing here for you to be involved with. Please go back to your own home."

"Your father and I built this house when we moved here from Pennsylvania. We borrowed money from the bank and worked night and day on this farm in order to pay back those loans. It's as much our house as yours."

They'd had to borrow money from the bank instead of family like most Amish? Viola barely had a chance to share a look with Elsie when their father replied.

"Yes, but you no longer live here. Mother, your place is in the back. Especially right now."

"Your brother Jacob wouldn't speak to me like this."

"Jacob also wouldn't live with you. He's out in Indiana! Neither would Sam. Or Aden. Or Sara. Matter of fact, no one wanted to live here in this big drafty *haus* with way too many bad memories."

Hurt flashed across her face, but her tone was sharp. "Then why did you?"

"Duty." He said the word like it was a curse word. Like it was something he couldn't ever push aside, no matter what.

If he'd meant to hurt Mommi, Viola saw that he'd done a good job of it. She paled.

But she didn't back away.

As the tension in the room thickened, their mother grabbed their father's arm. "Peter, stop. Stop saying such hateful things."

He shrugged off her grip. "They're only hateful if they're not true, Marie. And you know as well as I that I speak the truth."

Tears filled their mother's eyes. "I'm sorry, Lovina. Peter is not himself—"

Her eyes narrowed. "And we all know why, don't we?"

"No, I am very much myself, Marie," Peter countered. "And after more than forty years of keeping my mouth shut, I think I have every right to speak my mind." Still staring at his mother, he continued, his voice almost completely void of emotion.

"And so that is how we all came to be living here together. That is why you got stuck with me, Mamm," he said with a trace of irony. "No one else could stand you any longer."

Right before their eyes, their steely grandmother seemed to shrink. She turned on her heel and walked out. Seconds later, they heard the back door close quietly.

"Peter, whatever is wrong with you? You shouldn't talk that way to your mother. You should never have said such things."

"Why not? It's what we've all been thinking."

"That doesn't mean it's right." As if she had forgotten that Viola and Elsie were standing right there, their mother pointed to the bottle of vodka, sitting on the kitchen counter like a symbol of all that had gone wrong in their family. "Drinking isn't right, either, Peter. And you hid it, too."

"Other people drink."

"But we don't. We don't drink and we don't smoke. We don't even drink wine for special occasions. It's not our way. But even more, you've been lying to me for quite some time." Her voice now curiously empty, she said, "Quite some time."

"You knew?"

She closed her eyes. "*Jah.* I knew. I'm as guilty as you, husband. I've been hoping if I pretended I didn't know what was happening, I wouldn't have to deal with it.

Or worse, I could pretend it wasn't happening."

"You are making too much of one liquor bottle."

"We both know this isn't the only one, Peter."

Furious, he turned and glared at his daughters. "What have you done? Viola, I put the blame for all of this firmly on your shoulders. Elsie would have never caused such a scene."

"Me?" Viola felt her eyes burn.

"That's not fair, Daed," Elsie said quietly. "One of us was bound to discover it. Either me or Viola or Roman. All we wanted was some answers."

"You came here to cause pain, daughter."

"*Nee!*" their mother fairly shouted. "It isn't Viola who brought this into our lives; she's only been the one strong enough to bring it out into the open."

"And you don't think there would have been a better way to act? She marched in here in order to cause trouble."

Her mother shook her head sadly. "Oh, Peter. Don't you understand? The problem isn't that you were found out. The problem is that you shouldn't have been drinking in the first place. And you shouldn't have been lying to us for months. When you brought that into our house, and hid it away, and drank in private and lied about it . . . you have gone against all of us. You need some help."

His expression slack, their father looked from Elsie to Viola to their mother, then he turned and walked out the front door. Into the snow and cold without a coat on.

"Daed? Daed, don't go. We should talk about this," Elsie called out.

Their *mamm* shook her head. "*Nee,* Elsie. Leave him be."

Beside her, Elsie tensed. Viola reached for Elsie's hand, who clung to it like it was a lifeline. And truly, it did feel as if their whole world had gone crazy. No one had ever spoken to another that way. The anger and disappointment was so strong it felt almost tangible.

Watching their mother, standing so still and rigid, there seemed to be nothing else to say.

"Come on," she whispered. Still holding her sister's hand, she led Elsie up the narrow stairs to their bedroom.

Usually, Elsie would have pulled her

hand away, always shying away from any overt help. But this time she held Viola's hand as tightly in her own.

Perhaps she realized that this time it was Viola who needed support? Somehow, she'd managed to make everything worse.

chapter eighteen

Muscles in his arms and shoulders pumping, Ed shoveled his driveway in a daze. Though he appreciated the exercise, he knew nothing could tear his mind away from the meeting he'd had at CAMA.

All last night, he'd read through the binders and contemplated what he wanted in his life. And prayed and prayed for guidance.

But this morning, he still felt as confused as ever. Around him, snowflakes increased in size, floating in the wind, determined to cover his coat in a thick white blanket. It was beautiful.

And so different, he was sure, from Belize.

Yes, the weather was bitterly cold, but his whole body felt numb, both from the news and his reaction to it.

Looking down the street, he spied John Miller's old house. If John was still there, Ed knew he would've been tempted to knock on his door and ask for advice, but sharing his dilemma with John wasn't the right thing to do. He needed to talk to his father about the job offer before he spoke to anyone else.

But since the roads were too dangerous to go up to Daybreak, he was homebound. He needed to light a fire, brew a fresh pot of coffee, and reread every page in the binders, and then figure out just what exactly he was contemplating saying no to.

And what he might be saying yes to instead.

Aggravated by his thoughts, he put a little extra muscle into his chore and increased his pace. Sweat began to trickle down the middle of his back and the muscles in his arms began to burn.

The slight pain felt good.

When his driveway was as cleared as it

was going to get with the snow still falling, he decided to clear off the sidewalk, too.

An hour later, when he finally leaned the shovel against the side of the house, he went inside and discovered little Gretta sprawled out on a carpet by the door. Spying him, she sleepily got to her feet, shook herself awake, and then trotted over, her tail wagging affectionately.

A lump grew in his throat as he knelt down to brush his hand down her soft red fur, then he let her go outside. As he expected, she did her business and was back inside lightning fast. Then he did exactly what he set out to do, and carefully arranged a fire, brewed a pot of coffee, and sat down with the binders in his lap.

With Gretta curled up in her bed beside him, he opened up the top binder, flipped past the cover page, and began reading.

Two hours later, he set them on the floor and closed his eyes. And then he began to pray.

Peter was sweeping out the tack room and berating himself for blaming his girls for his troubles when Marie came into the barn. He stilled, bracing himself for another round of pain. He knew Marie was upset with him, and he didn't blame her one bit. He was fairly sure that any charges she fired at him were deserved. He'd lied to her, and broken any number of the covenants of their marriage vows. He'd raised his voice to Elsie and Viola, and to his mother, too.

He'd sinned in many, many ways.

But instead of launching into accusations, she walked to the tack room, leaned against the door frame, crossed her arms over her chest, and stood silent. Watching him.

His mouth went so dry, he could have sworn it had been stuffed with cotton.

For a good two minutes, neither of them said a word. After glancing her way, he turned and continued brushing the broom across already clean cement. It was impossible to stand still.

All the while, Marie continued to stand quietly, her face expressionless. He could only imagine what she was thinking. If their places had been reversed, he knew he would be feeling hurt and anger toward her.

Finally, she spoke. "Shouldn't Roman be doing this?"

"Ah, Roman was up early, so I let him

have a few hours off. He wanted to walk over to see Miriam." Roman had also been particularly quiet—more so than usual. Peter knew his son was disappointed in his behavior. Though he hadn't entered the fray, Roman had overheard the whole commotion, but had kept on doing his chores.

That dimple in her cheek that he knew so well appeared. "Miriam? She is a sweet girl. Are they getting serious?"

"He doesn't say much to me about his romances. But if I had to guess? I'd say no, I don't think they are yet. He doesn't talk about her in that way." Well, not like he'd once talked about Marie. When they'd been courting, every sentence he uttered always returned back to her.

He shrugged. "I could be wrong, though."

Leaning against the woodwork again, she said, "I haven't gotten that feeling about the two of them, either."

He stilled. Holding the broom, he felt a bit like a scarecrow in a field—stuck in the hard ground, unable to move away. Frozen in one place when there was no wind.

"Isn't it something?" Marie said, her voice breaking the silence. "Our *kinner* are twenty-three and twenty-two. Not a one of them seems close to getting married anytime soon. Why, we were married and I was pregnant with Roman at twenty-two."

"*Kinner* do things on their own time now, I suppose."

She bit her lip, just as if he'd said something noteworthy. "*Jah,* I suppose you're right."

As she continued to stand there, so calmly, so patiently, he placed the broom against the wall. Slowly he approached, watching every expression on her face. If she flinched, he knew he'd back up immediately.

But he couldn't bear for the two of them to be so distant. "Marie, you can't know how sorry I am. That said, I know that telling you that I'm sorry will never be enough."

"You are wrong about that."

"What?"

"Apologizing will always be enough."

"You think so?"

"I know so, because I love you. But you must talk to me, Peter. When did you start drinking? And why?"

He looked at his feet, then forced himself

to raise his chin and look her in the eye. The time for hiding was long past. Yet he struggled with the words.

"Just talk to me, Peter," she coaxed. "That's all I want. Just talk."

He swallowed hard. "About seven or eight months ago, everything got to me. We had some trouble with one of the cows—" Now, as he said the words, he wished he could take them back. In the grand scheme of things, who really cared about cows?

"Cows?" A line formed on her brow. "I don't remember any problem . . ."

"It was nothing. I didn't tell you. Anyway, the cow was bawling something awful, she was feeling sickly. I'd been up with her all night, walking with her. When morning came, I was dirty and exhausted. All I wanted to do was go lie down." He struggled to continue, praying to find the right words so that she might understand how he had been feeling.

"However, when I was going upstairs I saw my parents in the kitchen. Daed asked what I was doing, and, like a fool, I told him."

"Oh dear," Marie murmured.

Peter couldn't believe it was possible, but he found himself smiling. "Indeed. My father looked at me with contempt. And that forced me to think about how my *daed* had always gone through each day without complaint."

"That's probably not true . . ."

"Though I don't have to answer to them, I felt like I should defend myself. But suddenly, that felt like too much. So, even though I was exhausted, I showered and left for town. All I wanted to do was sit somewhere and just close my eyes. I ran to the store to pick up some food, and I saw a small bottle of vodka. And, remembering years ago, when me and my buddies used to sneak liquor and beer during *rumspringa* . . . I bought it." He winced; even to his ears, the explanation sounded weak.

"And you drank it?"

"I had a few sips. But the burning in the back of my throat seemed to numb my brain. And though I was still tired and stressed and worried, I didn't feel like I was incapable anymore." He shrugged. "I didn't start out wanting to become an alcoholic, Marie. I meant to throw that bottle away. I never had any intention of drinking again. But instead of tossing it in the trash, I kept it."

Even as he heard his words, he ached to take them back. He sounded pitiful. So pitiful.

He braced himself for her recriminations.

But instead, next thing he knew, she had launched herself toward him, her arms around his shoulders, her face hidden in the crook of his neck. Gently, he wrapped his arms around her and held her close. Her soft tears trickled down his neck, making his shirt damp, breaking his heart.

"I'm sorry, Marie," he rasped. "I never intended for you to find out. And I never intended to continue. I never meant to be this man that I've become."

"You are a *gut* man, Peter. You just need some help."

"I don't need any help. I just need to stop drinking."

Pure compassion entered her eyes. "If I ask you some questions, will you answer me truthfully?"

"I'll do my best."

"All right. Here's the first one. What do

you think would have happened if Viola and Elsie hadn't found that bottle under our sink?"

His answer was as painful as it was instant. "I would have continued to drink."

"Did you want to lie to me?"

"Of course not."

"Then, did you intend to hurt me?"

"*Nee,* Marie." His voice cracked.

"Then why did you never stop on your own?"

"I didn't think I was hurting anyone."

"You were hurting yourself."

"That's not the same." Bracing himself, he attempted to put his darkest thoughts into words, in a way that wouldn't sound pathetic, but would help his wife understand the depth of his confusion and anguish. "Marie, it's like this, you see. I thought if you never found out, it didn't make any difference. As long as I didn't hurt you. . . ."

"You only cared about hurting me?"

"You're everything to me. I love my parents, and I love our children. But you, Marie, are the one who holds my heart. I couldn't bear to cause you pain."

He watched her visibly struggle to make

sense of his words. He knew her so well and realized she was struggling to differentiate her feelings from his.

After a moment, she sighed. "I love you, Peter. As much love as you feel for me, I feel the same for you. Even if you lie or withhold things to protect me, I still feel the pain, because it's your pain I concern myself with." She cleared her throat. "Don't you see? Your feelings aren't that different from mine. Let me help you. Let me ask the bishop for help. He can guide us, I feel sure of it."

Bishop Coblentz was a good man. They'd known each other all their lives. But letting him know what he'd been doing would make his humiliation complete. "Let's not."

"But why? He won't betray you."

Even if the bishop never said a word about it, that knowledge would always be in his eyes. "I don't want him to know."

"I think you need help."

"You've already helped a lot, Marie. I'll stop on my own."

Hurt filled her eyes. "Peter, I know this hurts to hear, but you might not be able to stop on your own. And I might not be able to help you enough."

His frustration in himself finally transferred to his tone of voice. "Just give me a chance first, wouldya?" he snapped. "I know I've disappointed you, but I am still a man. And I am still capable of making decisions in this house." When she looked fearful, he reached out to her, just like she'd done to him a few minutes earlier. "Trust me, Marie. I don't want to lose you, and I don't want to keep secrets from you. I can do this."

"But if you can't . . ."

To placate her, he nodded. "If I can't, I'll let you know. And then you can ask the bishop for help."

"Promise?"

Her eyes were luminous, so filled with trust. With hope, too. He loved seeing that look in her eyes. He loved seeing her belief in him. "I promise."

When her lips curved upward in a small, tired smile, he felt his body relax. Unable to stop himself, he pulled her into his arms, smiling with contentment when she rested her head on his shoulder, just as she had for more than twenty years.

Just as she had back when they were eighteen and he'd taken her for a buggy ride in the cold and she'd first cuddled up next to him.

Holding her now, remembering how blessed they were to have each other, he promised himself yet again not to do anything to hurt her. He needed to continue to be the man she'd fallen in love with.

The man she needed him to be.

So yes, he was going to change his ways.

Or at the very least . . . make sure she never found out about his drinking again.

Wednesday evening

For about the hundredth time, Lorene felt like pinching herself. Here she was, sitting comfortably at John Miller's table, while he bustled in the kitchen to plate their food.

"Almost ready!" he called out.

He'd already said those same words several times. "Are you sure I canna help you?"

"You're my guest, Lorene."

"That doesn't mean I can't help you."

"It does to me." Something clanked, he

muttered something, then he spoke loudly again. "Almost ready."

Because he couldn't see her, she chuckled softly. This was the most entertained she'd been in years, and they hadn't even sat down together yet! "John?"

"I'm here," he said from the doorway, his hands laden with two bowls of soup. "I'm sorry it took me so long. I haven't quite mastered the skill of getting everything done at the same time."

"That's hard for me to do, too. Though I have to tell you that I haven't cooked many meals like this," she admitted as he set the plate in front of her with a pleased expression. As the scents of well-seasoned soup and rolls made her mouth water, she smiled. "It smells heavenly."

"Let's hope it takes just as good."

That's what she liked about him, Lorene realized. By all counts, John Miller had become successful. He owned his own store, bought a lovely home, and had taught himself to cook. But somehow he'd retained his modesty. He still looked as eager for her acceptance as he had ten years ago.

After sharing a silent prayer, they dug in.

And, of course, the meal tasted as wonderful as it looked. "It's great," she said. "Thank you, John."

"You know that I'm the thankful one, Lorene. Never did I imagine that we'd be together again."

They'd both been too full of pride. If she'd come to him years ago and told him that she'd changed her mind—or if he'd fought harder for their relationship—they might have enjoyed hundreds of meals like this.

"I never imagined it, either," she said. "I'm sorry for how long it took for us to come to our senses."

He set his soup spoon down. "Me, as well. But there's something we can do now, you know." Looking at her directly, he said, "We can promise that things will be different this time. That we'll be completely honest with each other."

Here was her chance. "I promise."

His expression turned wry. "You don't even need to think about it?"

"Not even for a minute."

Reaching out, he grasped her hand. "I don't need to think about it, either. I love you, Lorene. I can promise you that."

"I love you, too," she said simply. She

couldn't believe how simple it was. She loved him. Always had. She couldn't believe how nice it felt to hold his hand. To look into his eyes and see his promises.

It was so nice, Lorene let his delicious soup cool in its bowl. Virtually ignored.

chapter nineteen

Yesterday, Edward had wondered if it would ever stop snowing. The flakes had become so heavy and thick that branches, telephone lines, and electrical lines were in danger of breaking. The foul weather had suited his mood, however. He, too, felt like he was in the middle of his own storm, desperately attempting to find his way through a future that was hard to see.

Fancifully, he'd compared himself to an early explorer, trying to imagine what his life would be like if he took a different track. If he took a different route.

Now, though, he knew that he couldn't

be a solo traveler. He needed other people by his side to help him make his decisions.

This morning when he'd woken up, he'd leapt out of bed, his mind totally focused on his plans for the day. He needed to speak to his father, needed to show him the binder and get his advice. And he ached to talk to Viola, as well.

Viola!

What was it about her that kept drawing him in? The day before, as he'd watched the neighbor children run down their driveway in small sleds and build a snowman, his mind kept returning to memories of doing the same thing.

And thoughts of one day watching his children doing that as well. More than once, he'd imagined Viola being by his side.

And more than once he realized that he needed to include her in his deliberations.

Though there was a very good chance she wouldn't approve of him leaving again, he now knew her well enough that she would put her feelings aside to help him talk through all the pros and cons. Only then would she share her opinion. And he had no doubt that she would share it freely, and with great emotion.

Viola was like that, he realized with a grin. She was far from a shy woman, hesitant to share her views. He found her willingness to be bold completely enchanting. She was like no woman he'd ever met, and when he was around her, he found himself wondering if she was the woman God had intended for him.

By eleven, he felt he was in the right frame of mind to go to the retirement home and talk things over with his father. And to do the same with Viola if the occasion arose. He put on his old, thick boots, a sweater, and his coat and hat, and made his way to the retirement home.

A half hour later, he arrived.

"Edward, look at you!" Nancy, the receptionist, teased. "You look like the abominable snowman!"

"I feel like it, for sure. The sun is peeking out, but the temperature is probably not out of the teens."

"I fear you're right." She pointed to the cloakroom off the main lobby. "Feel free to hang your things up, or to leave them on. Whatever suits you."

"Danke." He went ahead and hung up his hat and coat, walked down the carpeted

halls that were becoming familiar, and finally knocked on his father's door. When no
one answered, he knocked again.

After another two minutes, his *daed* finally answered. His nose was red and
chapped, and his eyes were watering.
"Edward," he said around a cough.

All thoughts of Belize and Berlin fled in
an instant. "Daed, what's wrong?"

He waved off his concern. "I've got a
cold, that's what's wrong."

"Maybe it's the flu." He raised his hand,
ready to feel his father's forehead, when
his father cut off his motion with a fierce
glare. "No son of mine is going to start
feeling me for a fever."

"Would you like me to call for a nurse?"

"Definitely not. It's simply a winter cold,
Edward. It ain't nothing all of us have had
at one time or another."

"Ah."

"Did you come by simply to visit? Because if you did, I'm afraid I'm not much
for company right now."

"You don't need to be good company,
Daed. I'll just sit with you." Looking around
the dimly lit room, at the drawn curtains,
he said, "Would you like to play cards? Or

do you want me to open the curtains and let a little light in?"

"Ed, I was in bed. Half-asleep."

"Ah." Now he felt ill at ease. He'd come over for advice, but his father was obviously hoping his son would leave him in peace very soon.

Peering at him through bleary eyes, his *daed* gave him a knowing look. "You look like you've got something on your mind. That true?"

"Yes. I did want to speak to you about something, but it can wait."

"What's going on? Is there something wrong with the house?"

"No, no. Nothing like that." He backed away. "Listen, I'll call you tomorrow and see how you're feeling."

"That sounds *gut*." He was leaning back against his pillows and closing his eyes even as Ed turned the doorknob to walk out the door.

When he was out in the hall, he sighed. He'd been selfishly counting on his father's time and attention, and to see Viola, too. Now he had no reason to conveniently "run" into her. She was probably busy working, anyway.

With less than forty-eight hours left to make a decision, it looked like he was simply going to have to deal with this on his own.

He was still stewing as he put back on his winter coat and stocking hat and was walking outside. He was so preoccupied that he practically ran into Viola on the front sidewalk.

"You look like you're carrying the weight of the world on your shoulders, Edward Swartz," she said.

Viola, too, was bundled up. She wore a thick black wool cloak and a black bonnet on her head. The black made her skin look even more creamy than usual, her already rosy cheeks flushed from the cold.

"That's because it feels like it, Viola Keim."

Concern lit her pretty brown eyes. "Is something the matter?"

"No. It's just a problem that I'm working on. I'll get through it. I was going to talk to my *daed* about it, but he's feeling under the weather."

Reaching out, she gripped his arm. It was a sweet reminder of how much she, too, cared about his father. "I hope it's nothing serious."

"I asked him if he wanted the doctor. He assured me that it was only a cold." He shrugged. "I hope that's all that it is."

She visibly relaxed . . . but didn't remove her hand. "Mrs. Ames said several people have colds right now."

Liking her touch, he shifted his arm so he could hold her hand instead. "So . . . did you stay home yesterday?"

"I did. The roads were too rough."

"And did you enjoy yourself?"

She bit her lip before replying. "To be honest, no. I'm afraid things aren't all that happy at my house right now."

"Ah. It sounds like we both have a lot on our minds." Remembering that she was on her way into work, he smiled gently. "Have a good day, Viola."

"Wait. Do . . . Do you want to talk now? I have time. I mean if you have time, too. They don't need me to work today after all. I'm only here to pick up a paycheck."

"Sure," he said before chickening out. Of course he was worried about how she would react to his dilemma. But he was even more worried about the prospect of keeping his problem to himself for another day.

She flashed a smile. "I'll be right back."

Good to her word, she wasn't longer than five minutes. When she was by his side again, he pointed to a new fancy coffee shop on the corner. "How about we chat there?"

"Do you drink those fancy lattes?"

"*Nee,* a good cup of coffee is fine for me. But it looks quiet. And I have been known to enjoy strong coffee. A person gets used to such things in Central America."

She chuckled. "And here I thought you only ate rice and beans."

"And tortillas." His mouth watered as he remembered the taste of homemade tortillas, fresh from the oven. "I'll always remember that food fondly."

As they walked the two blocks, he told her stories about living in the mission compound.

Viola, to his surprise, looked interested instead of judgmental. Almost as if she was trying to imagine such a life. That gave him hope.

After ordering their coffees, black and plain coffee for him, a mocha latte with whipped cream for her, they sat down at a table by the window.

Viola closed her eyes when she sipped

her coffee. "I don't know why I like these fancy coffees so much, but I do."

His heart warmed as he eyed her. She had such a content look on her face, reminding him to take the time to appreciate the small pleasures in life more often.

Leaning back, she laughed. "Goodness, I think I've already finished half the drink."

He smiled, too. Then, before he could stop himself, he reached across and wiped the trace of whipped cream that had settled on her upper lip.

She stilled at his touch . . . and, perhaps, her gaze heated a bit.

"Whipped cream," he said. Needlessly. When her eyes widened, he took an overlarge sip of his piping hot coffee and nearly burned his tongue off.

Now it was her turn to look at him contemplatively. After another sip, she said, "What's on your mind, Edward?"

He didn't bother to hedge. "I got a call from CAMA, Christian Aid Ministries Association, last week. They asked that I visit with them on Tuesday."

"Is that unusual? I thought you were on vacation."

"It is a bit out of the ordinary. But they're my employer, so I figured that they just wanted to keep in touch with me."

Around another sip, and a swipe of her tongue to mop off a stray blob of whipped cream, Viola said, "That makes sense . . ."

"It did, to an extent." He swallowed. Now that it was time to tell the full story, he felt himself tense a bit. "I went into the meeting sure that the director simply wanted another report on my experiences at the mission. Sometimes they want to check facts or reports against each other. It makes sense, since the main office needs to make sure all our donations are being handled in the best ethical way."

"Was there a problem with your mission in Nicaragua?"

"Not at all."

"Then?"

He cleared his throat. "Actually, they made it sound like they were very happy with everything that I'd been doing . . ."

"So what did they want?"

"They want me to start another mission in Belize."

She wrinkled her nose. "Where's Belize?"

"Off the coast of Central America. Near Guatemala and Honduras."

She still didn't look concerned. "Well, it's nice that they already know where to place you one day. So, what's wrong? Do you not want to go to Belize?"

"It's not that. It was two things. First, it's a little too early in my career to be given such responsibility. I didn't expect it."

"Ah. Well, God never gives us a task we aren't ready for. Perhaps God and CAMA see leadership qualities in you."

"The folks on the board of CAMA said they did." He hoped sincerely that he wasn't sounding too full of himself. He didn't want this to be about pride and ego.

"I'm not quite sure why you look so agitated. I'm sure they'll help you."

"They will. But the problem is about the timing. They want me to accept or refuse the position by Friday."

"Next Friday?" When he shook his head, her eyes widened. "Tomorrow?" That one word was heavy with dismay.

"Yeah."

"Why the hurry?"

"The first person they had in mind can't

go anymore. I'm the second choice. If I accept, they want me to go out there next week to hire people and do an inventory of supplies."

Her eyes widened. "So soon?"

Miserably, he nodded. "This first trip would only be for about ten days, then I'd come back here. But it would only be until they got everything together. At the most, it would be about two weeks."

"Two weeks," she echoed.

"Yes." Uncomfortable, he spit out the rest of the news. "Then, well, they'd want me to go out there for five years."

"Edward, you told me most assignments were only for a year or two at a time."

"That is still true. But because I would be the director, and because the facility would be brand-new, they'd want me to take on a longer time."

He watched her process that. Little by little, the lines that had formed on her brow smoothed. "That makes sense."

"Yes."

"But I can hardly believe it."

He was still having a difficult time grasping the news himself. If another man told him that he'd been offered the chance to start up a new mission, Ed knew he'd be telling him to jump at the chance.

But all he could think about was everything he'd be missing. All that he'd be leaving behind.

Staring at his hands that were now curved around his mug, he added, "I might get to come home for a week's vacation during that time. But it's not a certainty."

"Five years is a long time."

He nodded.

"So, after next week, we might not see each other again for five years." Viola sounded defeated, almost as disappointed as he felt.

But her statement wasn't quite true. As he'd said, he'd be back. But it wouldn't be the same. When he did return, he'd be busy with meetings and phone calls and shopping and packing. If he had a few hours to spare each day, it would be spent with his father. "We wouldn't see each other much. I mean, unless you wanted to visit me."

She looked incredulous. "In Belize?"

"It's not the end of the earth, Viola."

"I didn't mean to sound like that." She

pushed her drink to one side. "Is there any way you can refuse the position?"

"I could." When he saw her worried expression ease, he knew he needed to tell her more. "But, Viola, I'm not sure if I want to refuse it."

"But if you weren't the first choice, I imagine they have others in mind."

She was making it sound like he was easily replaceable, and perhaps he was. But it still stung his pride. He tried not to let his hurt show. "There are many others in the organization who they could've asked. They chose me. They prayed about it, read my reports, and talked to people who had been in the field with me. Only then did they ask me. It's an honor to be asked." He knew he sounded full of himself, but he couldn't help it. Even if she didn't agree with him, he wanted Viola to understand that the position hadn't been offered lightly.

"I see."

Ed could almost see her wrapping a cold, hard shell around herself. "No, I don't think you do. I feel really torn, Viola. I just came back to Berlin. After feeling vaguely like a visitor in my own home, I'm finally settling into living in America again. I'm seeing my father daily, and I love seeing him."

"I understand . . ."

"But if I push this off and refuse, I know I'll feel guilty. And I'll worry that the Lord had meant for me to take this position, but that I refused it for my own selfish reasons."

She blinked. "That would be difficult, I suppose . . ."

But she still seemed distant. As if she'd been hoping he'd say something more. And so though it was surely too early to confide in her, he forged ahead. "And there's more. There's you."

"Me? What do I have to do with anything?"

It was time. Time to take a step forward, time to let the feeling that was running through him override all his doubts and worries. "A lot. I've been thinking about you a lot."

"I'm sorry. I . . . I don't understand."

He knew she didn't. And honestly, he was struggling, too. He felt just as conflicted about his relationship with her and the future he wanted with her as he did about everything else. He wasn't a man who liked to rush decisions or rush to judgments.

But he didn't have time to wait. He knew his feelings for her were impacting his decision or at least how he felt about the opportunity. "The truth is that I've grown to really appreciate our friendship, Viola."

"I, as well," she said slowly.

Since she looked just as stunned by the fact that she was opening up as well, it gave him the strength to continue. "Since we're being so honest, I suppose I need to tell you that more than once I've entertained thoughts of there being something more than just friendship between us."

"What do you mean by 'more'?"

She had to know what he meant! But perhaps she needed to hear the words? Though it was painful, he continued, feeling the whole time like he was precariously perched on the edge of a cliff. "More, as in I want to have a deeper relationship with you." Even as he heard himself, he wanted to slap his words away. He sounded awkward and childish.

He was a man. If he could attend to hundreds in a foreign country, surely he could manage to describe his feelings to one petite woman with brown eyes?

"Let me try this again. What I'm trying to say is that I really like you. I want to court you." *Ach*, but his collar suddenly felt as if it were choking him. "It's true," he added, for good measure.

But it looked as if Viola Keim was determined to have everything he said written out as clear as day. "Court, as in marriage?"

"Yes." His whole body felt hot. Could he be any more of a stumbling fool? Goodness, but he'd always imagined that he'd feel more sure of himself when he fell in love.

Her eyes wide, she whispered, "Edward, I don't know what to say."

He felt so twisted inside, he couldn't resist teasing her. "You always know what to say."

Her lips curved up slightly before pressing together in consternation. "Thirty minutes ago, I might have agreed with you about having a future. Now? I'm not so sure."

Feeling lower than an ant at a picnic, he wondered if the Lord had encouraged him to speak so he could put all hope of a future with Viola out of his mind. Now what he really needed to do was slink away and hope that he didn't see her alone anytime soon. "Viola, I'm sorry for speaking my mind like I did. I can see that you're uncomfortable. I hope I haven't embarrassed you too much."

She shook her head. "I'm not embarrassed. I have to admit, that I, too, have felt some of the very same things that you have. I'd really hoped you'd be here long enough for us to figure them out."

"I didn't go looking for this opportunity. And I don't even know if I'm going to take it."

"But you might."

"Yes. I might."

She pulled her drink toward her and took another sip. And then another one. "May I ask you a question?"

"Of course. Ask all the questions you want. I really need your help to figure out what to do."

"Well, are any of the missionaries, um, married?"

"Some."

"And do their wives and husbands go there, too?"

"Some. Others stay behind."

"Truly?"

Now that they'd come so far, he ached to pepper her with questions. Was she hinting that she would want to go with him? Or was she using this as another excuse to show that they weren't meant to be together?

"Some wives don't feel comfortable living out of the country, or they don't feel comfortable raising their *kinner* on foreign soil," he admitted. "So they stay behind."

"Ah."

He didn't know what that meant. He was in over his head. He'd started the conversation with selfish motives. He'd needed someone to listen to him, to help him weigh his options. But suddenly, they were not only discussing whether or not he would go, but their future.

Standing up, he said, "I'm sorry. This wasn't what I intended to happen."

She stood up as well, a small smile on her lips. "What did you intend?"

"I don't know. I went to Daybreak to see my father. Now I've told you far too much." He backed away. "I need to go." He pulled his coat on. "I'll walk you back home."

"*Nee,* I'm going to go see my aunt Lorene. She lives in town."

"I'll walk you there, then."

"I don't need you to do that." Resting her fingers lightly on his arm, she said, "Perhaps we could continue this discussion sometime soon."

"Um," he said, before he turned away. Then practically raced down the sidewalk in the opposite direction.

And realized only after a few minutes that he had no idea where he was walking to. After a moment's pause, he continued.

It seemed fitting that his feet were in the same mind-set as his head.

chapter twenty

Viola discovered if she concentrated only on trying not to fall while walking on the slick sidewalk that she could neatly push aside the whirlwind that was taking place in her head.

Five minutes went by. Ten. She stopped at an intersection, then hurriedly crossed when the signal told her she could. She kept her head lowered in order to keep her eyes from getting the worst of the wind.

But, of course, no matter how much she tried to avoid it, her brain buzzed with snippets of her conversation with Edward. She felt a sense of loss and hope all at the same time. For most of her life, she'd wondered why no other men in her community had ever created a pattering in her heart like Ed seemed to. For years, she'd wondered if something was wrong with her insides, that perhaps love and marriage and children weren't in her future. That God had intended for her to always look out for Elsie.

But now it seemed as if God had intended for her to experience love and romance and giddiness, too. It just happened to be with a man whom she shouldn't have looked twice at. Edward Swartz was altogether wrong for her.

But what was she going to do when he was gone? She had no idea. Already it felt as if her heart was breaking, and she hadn't even decided if she wanted to see him again.

But he liked her. And moreover, it seemed as if he wanted to spend his life with her. He definitely had talked courting and marriage.

It was all so overwhelming. But at the same time, she felt as if she'd been gifted with the most wonderful of surprises. And she wanted to hold that feeling close to her chest and keep it to herself.

What was she going to do? She could only imagine how her parents would react if she wandered in their house and announced that she planned to marry Edward Swartz and become a missionary's wife in Belize.

Her parents would probably team up with her grandparents and lock her in her room. She didn't know if she would blame them, either. Why, she had no idea where Belize was! It had been all she could do to keep a straight face when Ed had mentioned that it was near Guatemala and Honduras. Those countries sounded just as strange and unfamiliar.

She needed a geography lesson, not a marriage proposal!

Stewing on it all, Viola couldn't think of another person in the world who would understand what she was struggling with better than her aunt Lorene. She hoped she would be home.

When she arrived at Lorene's house, she took care to only step on the salted areas so she wouldn't slip.

Lorene opened the door before she could knock. "I'm so glad to see you," she said.

Pulling her inside, she gasped. "Your hands are like ice. And your cheeks are bright red! Have you been walking outside for hours? Come into the kitchen and I'll give you some tea." She paused. "Or wouldja rather have coffee?"

Coffee could now only remind her of sitting with Edward. "Tea would be *gut*."

"Tea it is." Lorene hummed softly as she filled her kettle with water and set it to boil.

Viola watched her with interest. Her favorite aunt's cheeks glowed and she seemed to be almost bursting with good spirits. "You seem happy."

"Oh, I am. Take off your cloak and sit down."

She did as her aunt asked, but kept her eyes on Lorene. No, she hadn't been mistaken. Lorene wore a smile as big as Texas. "Is there a particular reason you're so happy?"

Lorene glanced at her over her shoulder. "You mean why can't I stop smiling even though our family is practically falling apart at the seams?"

"Pretty much."

Lorene's expression softened. "Are you

doing all right? Elsie called me and told me about Peter. I'm sure it was difficult to learn about your father's drinking."

She nodded. "Did you suspect?"

"*Nee.* And though I am worried about him, I am not that surprised," she added after a moment's hesitation.

"Why not?"

"Peter has always been the type of man to try to keep a calm outer shell. But sometimes that isn't the best way to solve one's problems. All covering up your feelings does is give way to the temptation to pretend that they don't exist." With a wry expression, she added, "Believe me, I know this to be true. I've tried to hide underneath a happy shell."

"Mamm said that she talked with him." Viola ached to say more, about how angry her father had been with her. And how upset she and Elsie had been. And how it had even felt as if their mother wasn't on their side. But revealing those things felt vaguely like a betrayal.

And she now had even more things to think about. Things, she suddenly realized, that had to do with planning her future, not her family's. "Lorene, tell me your good news."

"Oh, I will. Just give me a moment to finish brewing us tea. I made cookies, too. Sour-cream cutouts."

"They sound delicious." And they did sound *wunderbaar*. If she'd thought she could eat. Which she didn't.

"Oh, they are," Lorene said with a smile. "I sampled a few just to make sure."

In no time at all, a pretty china teapot was on the table, along with two white tea-cups decorated with soft pink flowers. There was a matching plate filled with heart-shaped cookies, as well. Heart shaped!

But what drew her attention the most was her aunt. Lorene was sitting across from her, her cheeks flushed and her eyes bright. She looked younger and happier than Viola could ever remember her being.

"Lorene, I canna take it anymore. What happened?"

"I've fallen in love, all over again."

"With John Miller?"

"Of course." She picked up her teacup, then abruptly set it right back down, as if even thinking about sipping a hot brew was too distracting. "Last night, I went to John's house and he cooked me dinner."

"That sounds romantic."

"It was. He made me soup and we promised that we'd do things differently now." Lorene sighed, looking out into the distance, like she was in her own world. "Oh, Viola, I can't tell you how happy I am. It's the most amazing feeling in the world to know that the man you love loves you back."

"He told you that he loved you?"

"But of course." She looked at her strangely. "Viola, I'm not playing here. This thing we're feeling? It's serious. John and I aim to marry soon."

"Soon?"

"As soon as possible."

"What about Mommi? I thought she didn't approve of him."

"That hardly matters anymore."

"Because she kept her own secrets?"

"Partly." Shrugging, she added, "I think it's also because I grew up. Finally. I stopped worrying about what my parents wanted me to be and started concentrating on what I wanted, and what I thought God was wanting for me."

This was just what Viola needed to hear. Leaning forward, she said, "Don't you think it's hard to know what He wants?"

"I used to think so," Lorene said after a moment's pause. "I used to think that hearing his word was going to be like hearing a voice over my shoulder. Of feeling a nudge from behind. But now I'm realizing that I simply had to be open to His will. I realized that He put John and me together again. That this was our time. Thank goodness for you and Edward Swartz!"

Hearing her name linked with Ed made her feel a little awkward, as if Lorene had suddenly read her mind. "Ed and I didn't do anything."

"Well, I wouldn't have gone to Daybreak if you weren't working there. And John wouldn't have been there if Atle wasn't living there. And of course, Atle wouldn't have been living there if Ed hadn't decided to listen to the Lord and go on a mission trip. Of course God put all that in motion." She chuckled softly. "Viola, I got nowhere on my own for ten years!"

Viola supposed her aunt had a point. But Lorene sounded so sure. So convinced!

Was God really in charge? Did everything happen for a reason? Had the Lord been moving all of them in one another's path in order to do his will?

It just felt too simple. Surely falling in love was supposed to be harder?

"When are you going to tell the family about you and John?"

"One night this week. John has quite a bit of work to do . . . and I wanted things to quiet down with Peter and my *mamm* a bit before I sprung this on them."

"I hope no one will tell you that you can't marry him now."

"No one will, Viola. Because I won't accept that pronouncement. This time, I'm determined to live my own life, and I care only about pleasing the Lord, not the dozen people in our family."

"But it's not always that easy."

"I agree. But between you and me? I think I made love and marriage too hard. I cared more about earning my parents' approval instead of feeling certain that they loved me no matter what."

The words made sense.

As did Lorene's firm, positive attitude. Viola slumped, feeling more confused than ever. What was wrong with her? Obviously, Lorene had embraced the right things—

how could something wrong make her feel so happy?

But if falling in love was simply a matter of racing ahead, even if a person knew it would cause others pain?

She wasn't sure if that was for her.

Slowly, she stood up. "I think I'm going to go on home now."

"Wait a minute. You just got here." She pointed to the beautiful snack she'd laid out for them. "And you haven't touched the cookies and barely sipped any tea."

"I know. I'm sorry."

Lorene tilted her head to one side, looking at her more carefully. "Viola, did you want to speak about something? Is something bothering you?"

She didn't want to ruin Lorene's *wonderful-gut* news. She didn't want to burden her aunt with problems that she wasn't even sure she had.

That wasn't the type of person she wanted to be. That, at least, was something she was sure about.

"Nothing's bothering me."

"I fear you're lying."

"If I'm lying, it's because what's on my mind is nothing of importance. And it's nothing that a good long walk won't take care of. I think I really need the fresh air to clear my head."

"I can understand that," she said slowly. "But even small problems can be difficult to solve by yourself. I'm happy to help."

"And I know that. But I'll be fine." Reaching out, she gave her aunt a fierce hug, then turned away before she gave in to temptation and shared too much.

And, as she began the long walk home, Viola realized she'd been correct. She needed the time to clear her head and to think. To imagine a life with Edward Swartz. And to contemplate a life without him, too.

Later that afternoon, Lorene got in her buggy and went to Peter's. She was still thinking about Viola. She felt sure Viola was feeling conflicted about something and she had a feeling it was Edward Swartz. What could she do to help Viola not make the same mistakes that she had? Surely all her years of feeling afraid could be used to help Viola not make the same mistakes?

When she arrived on the property, Lorene drove the horse straight to the barn. Thankful that it was empty, she unhitched

Bonnie and walked her to a stall. She needed a few extra moments to gather her thoughts and figure out how to help Viola.

And, she realized, to try to find a way to forgive her mother. All the negative feelings she'd been holding tight to her heart weren't good for anyone. Even seeing the *dawdi haus* caused tension to rise up in her chest.

For almost ten years, she'd held tight to her worry and distress, afraid to let even the tiniest bit of her sadness come to light. Admitting disappointment never did anyone a bit of good. It didn't make the memories easier, or the sadness dissipate.

But hiding it also didn't remove the pain. It was still there. Festering.

But perhaps the past didn't matter so much anymore. It was over, and had only really affected her life and John's. Not the whole family's. No, all that had happened was that she'd become resigned to a lifetime living alone. And now, things would be different.

Roman entered the barn just as she was about to walk to the house. "Aunt Lorene, I would've unhitched Bonnie for you."

"I didn't mind."

"Will you be spending the night? If so, I'll go ahead and brush her and give her some feed."

"That's kind of you. I don't think I'll tackle the snowy streets in the dark tonight." Raising her chin so she could gage his expression a little easier, she realized that she'd been so focused on her nieces that she'd hardly spared a thought for her nephew. And it was Roman's way to let others claim the majority of the attention, too. "Hey, since we're alone, maybe you could tell me how you're doing."

"I'm fine," he said quickly.

"Of course you are, Roman," she teased. "I've never heard you say different."

"That's because it's the truth."

"I've noticed you haven't said much to anyone about what's been going on with your grandparents."

"Oh, that they're liars?" He pulled his hat lower on his head, shielding most of his expression from her view. "I'm glad I'm not involved. I don't really care what my grandmother was or used to be."

"You don't?" She found that hard to believe. She'd found herself thinking about her parents' deception almost every waking moment, and she knew her siblings felt the same way.

Lorene stayed by his side. "I'm afraid I can't say the same," she admitted. "Whenever I think about all the times my mother made me feel so worthless, I want to scream." She paused, then delved deeper. In for a penny, in for a pound. "And how are you doing with your *daed*'s revelation?"

"That he's been secretly drinking in the bathroom of the house?" He rolled his eyes. "I don't have much to say about that, either— except that it came as a surprise. I couldn't make up all this turmoil."

"Turmoil is a good way of describing it. But, I feel sure things will get better. We're all communicating now. That's a big improvement."

Roman shrugged. "The Bible says forgiveness is a virtue. I suppose I'll do my best to follow those words. They have to mean something, right?"

Both dismayed and a mite irritated that her nephew was quoting the Good Book to her, she nodded. "Of course."

"Then that's what we need to do."

Her nephew was one of the most gentle

Christian men she'd ever met. "I have a lot to learn from you."

Grinning, he shook his head in that self-deprecating way of his. "I don't know about that. I'm simply trying to do my best." Picking up a curry comb, he began brushing Bonnie. "Viola told me about you and John Miller. It seems we've got a wedding to throw as soon as possible." His smile grew. "Now that's a story I was mighty interested in."

"I just told Viola my news this afternoon! How in the world did she have time to already share it with you?"

"Oh, she managed. You know Viola. She doesn't have a shy or hesitant bone in her body."

"I believe the Bible talks about that, too," she said dryly.

He chuckled. "I'm sure it does. But Aunt Lorene, I think Viola had a good point."

"And what was that?"

"That it's good to have something to celebrate. Why be shy with good news?"

"I suppose you're right," she said. After all, they'd more than had their fair share of bad news lately!

"I know I am! You're a nice lady, Aunt Lorene. You deserve some happiness and romance. I'm glad you and John came to your senses. I mean, you sure didn't want to wait much longer."

"Yes, it would have been awful to wait until I was forty."

"Oh, to be sure."

The idea that he thought of forty years old as almost ancient amused her, though she recalled feeling much the same way when she was Roman's age.

"Lorene, are ya teasing me?"

"Only as much as you're teasing me." They shared a grin, reminding Lorene of how blessed she was to have Peter's children in her life.

"Well, I suppose we should go into the house. We can stand together if Elsie or Mamm starts to tell us about their secrets!"

"I hope we'll be strong enough to bear the news well." Unable to stop herself, she wrapped an arm around his shoulders and squeezed lightly. Roman did lighten her spirit. "It has to get better. I guess we'll see."

"Maybe I should start sleeping in the barn," Roman joked.

"Oh, I hope it wouldn't come to that. You can always stay with me or Sam. We'd all do whatever it took to make sure you three kids are happy."

He turned back to her, all traces of humor gone from his expression. "But that's the problem, Aunt Lorene. See, we're not kids anymore. And we haven't been for a long time."

She was starting to realize that.

chapter twenty-one

Staring out her kitchen window, Lovina watched her grandson walk his horse through the back field. Two years ago, a local farmer had fallen on hard times and had asked Roman if he'd accept the horse as a gift. The farmer could no longer afford to feed the gelding, but was so attached to him that he worried more about the horse having a good home than getting any money for him.

Which, Lovina had privately thought, was a fitting example for why the farmer had been in financial trouble. If he'd simply sold the horse and moved on, he would have gotten rid of the animal and had some money in his pocket, too.

She'd mentioned as much to Peter. Though he said he agreed, he didn't stand in the way of Roman's gift.

"My boy loves animals, and has always wanted a horse of his own."

She had thought that was a rather poor reason to take on the expense of another horse. "Is it a worker?"

"Oh, *jah.* Chester will make a fine buggy horse. And he'll most likely ride it a bit, too. But that horse will also give him a lot of pleasure."

"An expensive way to make him happy."

Peter had simply shrugged. "Life is expensive, ain't so? Having *kinner,* paying for animals. And fuel, and food. One more horse won't make that much of a difference."

No matter how many times she'd try to make him see that he should be harder on his son, Peter had refused to yield to her point of view.

Now, as she watched Roman lead Chester by his bridle through the snow, stopping every now and then to rub a hand down his neck, Lovina had to admit that she hadn't seen anything as calming and peaceful as that in a long time. The horse seemed to appreciate the chance to stretch its legs, and the boy—who wasn't much of a boy anymore—looked just as happy to be away from the chaos of their house. It was obvious that the horse and that boy needed each other. Even to her.

Which, of course, brought her to thinking about what else she'd been wrong about over the years. Too many things to count.

The only thing she'd never regretted was leaving behind her old ways and adopting Amish ones. That had always felt right.

Turning away from the window, she leaned her head against the hard back of the wooden chair and tried to recall the moment she and Aaron had decided to keep her past a secret.

Had it been when she joined the church? Or earlier?

Maybe it had been when they'd both realized they'd done things that could never be erased. That seemed to be the far more reasonable explanation, she mused. Even as she realized she was lying to herself.

Here in the solitary confines of the small kitchen, she knew exactly when they'd decided to rewrite her past . . . when they moved from Lancaster County to Holmes. They'd decided when they moved to Ohio that they would reinvent her background, so as to not invite questions.

She'd been all for that. She had wanted to move to Ohio as Mrs. Aaron Keim, not as Lovina—a.k.a. Lolly—Johnson. She wanted to be known as the perfect Amish wife. Who always did the right thing.

The woman whom Aaron was proud to call his own.

Not Lolly, the impulsive, self-centered, vain girl she'd been.

It had been hard work, pretending to be something she was not. Early in their marriage, when she was particularly irritated with Aaron over something, she'd yearned to pick up the phone and cry to her mother.

Not that her mother would've been understanding at all. She'd disagreed with just about every decision she'd made about Aaron Keim. "You're going to regret this, Lolly," she warned. "You have no real idea about what is in store for you. The Amish aren't like us."

"Mom, you have no idea what you're

talking about. You don't know a single person who's Amish."

"I know Aaron."

"Aaron is a good man."

"He's far older than you."

"So?"

"He's had another life, Lolly. Pretending it doesn't exist doesn't change things." Her tone had held a thick note of frustration. There was much she wasn't saying, but that they both knew—that his first wife and child would always be in his heart. "A man can't help but compare the present with the past."

She'd secretly feared that, as well. Though no one else talked of it, Aaron had sat her down and told her the truth. All the truth.

During that hour, he'd encouraged her to be as nosy as she'd wanted. He wanted her to ask as many questions as she could. Because, he warned, when that hour was over, he didn't intend to ever discuss it again.

So she'd asked. And she'd smiled. And she'd pretended to herself and her mother that the mere hour Aaron had allotted her had been enough.

But it hadn't.

A timid knock on her door jerked her to her feet. "Yes?" she called out.

"Mommi, it's Elsie."

"Come in, child." Her heart softened as she watched her granddaughter quietly enter the room. As always, Elsie had on her thick glasses. The heavy lenses magnified her brown eyes, but didn't seem to help all that much. Though Elsie bore her disability stoically, Lovina feared that it was just a matter of time before she lost her eyesight completely. "And how are you today?"

Elsie wore a wry smile. "Truthfully? Not so well. I'm worried about Daed."

"I am, too. Come sit down." Hesitantly she reached out to her granddaughter to guide her to the chair.

Elsie shrugged off her hand. "I'm not blind. Yet."

"I know."

She sat down and waited. Lovina wasn't too good at this. She'd raised her six children by being strict and firm. She'd always thought no good came from coddling them.

She treated Viola and Roman much the same way.

But with Elsie? The girl brought out a tenderness from deep inside her that she hadn't realized existed. Or, truth be told, she'd more likely hidden it deep inside herself. With Elsie, she wanted to protect the girl, and comfort her, too. And it wasn't just Elsie's disability that caused her to be like this. No, it was more Elsie's calm demeanor. It was soothing and gentle, as if God had given her all the best qualities from the rest of the family to make up for her failing eyesight.

"Mommi, I don't know what to think about Daed."

"I suppose not." She opened her mouth to relay once again how disappointed she was in Peter, but held her tongue. Her criticisms wouldn't ease Elsie's mind. "Would you like a cup of coffee?"

"I'm fine. I really just came over here to see if you needed anything."

"I don't need anything." It was true; she didn't. She only had a lot of "wants"—for things she couldn't change.

"Grandmother, do you think I'll ever find love?"

Elsie couldn't have surprised her more if she'd suddenly picked up a book and started reading it. "What makes you think about love, child?"

"I'm not a child. I'm the same age as Viola, you know. And you never call her 'child.'"

"I don't mean it how it sounds. It's only a habit," she countered. "But let's concentrate on you. What has made you think about love?"

"Viola. I think she's in love."

"With Edward Swartz?"

"Jah." Elsie smiled sheepishly. "Mommi, she's really head over heels."

Hearing the English phrase that had been so popular when she was a teenager almost made her smile. "That's kind of sudden, don'tcha think?" she said lightly.

"Yes, but she told me that she can't help herself."

Lovina had been like that. When she'd fallen in love with Aaron, she'd practically leapt to a life with him. No difference in their ages or backgrounds had mattered. "I suppose we'll all see what God has in mind for them."

Elsie's brows arched over her glasses. "That's all you have to say?"

"You expected more?"

"Jah," she said slowly. "I thought for sure that you'd share your opinion."

"Sharing too much has gotten me into

trouble lately. What does your mother say?"

"Mamm? Oh, she doesn't know about this. There's no way Viola would tell her. Mamm would want to talk about all the pros and cons for hours."

That did sound a bit like Marie. Peter's wife had always been one to carefully think things through. Since she wasn't anxious to become embroiled in yet another problem in the house, she returned the conversation to Elsie. "If you aim to fall in love and have a man of your own, I guess you should keep your eye out." Of course, the moment she said the words, she winced. "Sorry. Poor choice of words."

To her relief, Elsie chuckled. "I know what you mean. So, Mommi, you think it's easy to fall in love?"

"*Nee.* I don't think it's easy at all. Finding a partner for life ain't easy. We all have good points and bad. Finding someone who is compatible is challenging, for sure."

"Is that what you did? You looked for compatibility?"

Lovina started to nod but stopped herself. "*Nee.* That's not what I did. I fell headfirst into love with your grandfather. So much so, I was willing to go against my parents and my friends in order to have a life with him."

Elsie sighed. "That's what I want. The kind of love where you don't have a choice but to follow your heart."

"I hope you find it then."

"And you've had no regrets?"

The question hung in the air between them. Once again, Lovina realized she could be truthful or she could be as she'd always been.

"I've had no regrets," she said at long last.

Elsie smiled in relief before standing up and pressing a kiss to her cheek. "I'm glad we talked, Mommi," she said before walking back out the door.

"I am, too," Lovina whispered. And more than that? She was glad she'd decided to lie.

Because, of course, she had regrets. But if there was one thing she'd learned, it was that stewing over past mistakes did no one any good.

Herself least of all.

chapter twenty-two

"I didn't expect to see you today," his father said from across the darkened room. "Edward, I told you to stay away until I called you."

"But I didn't say I was going to do that."

After a stuffy sneeze, his father said, "You should listen to me. I'm still your father."

Ignoring that nonsense, Ed strode forward. "It's good I didn't listen and stopped by instead. You look worse, Daed. We need to get you to the doctor."

"I've already seen the *doktah*. He came by last night."

"Why last night?" Ed sat down on the side of the mattress. Even in the dim light, he could see his father's scowl. He couldn't recall his father ever liking to be fussed over, and it looked like some things never changed. "Why did he come last night? Did you get worse? You should have called me."

Before his father could answer, he continued. "Why didn't you call? I would've come over."

"For what purpose? So you could stand against the wall and watch me get my temperature taken?" He scowled. "That, *boo,* was the last thing I needed."

"Daed."

With a raspy, wet cough, his father sat up and glared at him when he attempted to fluff the pillows behind his head. "He came last night because I called him myself."

"And?"

"And, he told me to stay in bed and drink liquids."

"Oh."

"Oh, indeed." He coughed again. "Well, boy, since you're determined to keep me from resting in peace, I suppose we should talk. Turn on my lamp."

Ed did as he was asked, anxious to examine his father in a better light. After scanning his face, he eased. His father might have a thick cough, but his eyes looked clearer and his cheeks had a bit of color in them. "You do look a little better."

His father rolled his eyes. "*Danke.* Now, I have to say that you don't look well. In fact, you look like you have something on your mind. Do you?"

"Yeah. Daed, I need your advice."

His father's expression went from aggrieved to interested. "You do, huh?" He scanned the room with a frown. "Hmm. If you're coming over, looking for fatherly words of wisdom, I think I'd better get dressed."

"There's no need for that."

"There's every need. Now, go stand outside the door and wait for me. I'll be out in ten minutes."

Ed was tempted to argue, but decided to choose his battles. "All right."

"Good decision, Edward."

Taking up his post outside the door, Ed felt a bit silly, like a child awaiting a meeting with his teacher. However, there was a part of him that was relieved. Selfishly, he needed his father's attention, and they'd never had a serious conversation when his father was in his pajamas.

When his father came out, he looked pale, but smelled like soap and fresh laundry. "Let's go get some hot tea and talk, Edward."

"Should I go get your wheelchair?"

"*Nee*. I can walk still. A little bit of exercise might do me good."

Once again, Ed bit his lip to keep from offering an opinion.

When they sat down in yet another cozy room with a fireplace that was next to empty, Ed folded his hands on the table. Now that it was time, he hardly knew how to start.

"Best get it over with," his *daed* urged.

"All right." Looking squarely at his father, he said, "Earlier this week, I had a meeting with Mr. Cross. He's head of Christian Aid Ministries Association."

"And?"

"They want me to be the director of a mission in Belize." He squeezed his knuckles together and took a deep breath. "And they want me to go down there next week to start setting up things."

"That's sudden."

"I thought so, too."

"And when would you go down there for good?"

"Two weeks after that."

"Ah." The heavy coffee mug wobbled in his father's frail hands as he picked it up and sipped. Taking his time, he swallowed and took another sip.

Edward watched his father's Adam's apple move with each swallow, and reflected once again how many times they'd had much the same type of conversation. In the past, he'd usually been sharing good news.

Now, though, it felt as if he was letting his father down.

"I haven't told them I would go. But they need to know today if I refuse the offer."

"Are you thinking that you want to refuse? Is that what you want to do?"

"I don't know. That's why I wanted to speak to you."

He looked flummoxed. "This ain't my choice to make, Edward. It's yours."

"But your opinion matters to me."

"I'm glad of that. But you're a grown man, not a child. I'm not about to start telling you what to do. No matter what I say or think, the fact of the matter is you're going to have to deal with the consequences."

"I see." He felt curiously deflated. He'd hoped this conversation would erase all his questions and set him at ease.

His *daed*'s eyes softened. "So, I won't be telling you what to do. But I'll be glad to listen while you think this through. What are you thinking?"

"Too much," he said in a rush, he was so relieved to have a sounding board. "I don't know if I'm ready for the job. And I hadn't planned on being gone so soon." He paused. "I'll miss you, Daed. We've barely had time to get reacquainted."

"There weren't no need for us to get to know each other, Edward," he said dryly. His gaze sharpening, he said, "Is there any other reason? Any particular woman you're thinking of?"

"It's no secret that I've become fond of Viola Keim. But it's too early to know if our feelings are real."

Ed took a deep breath and went on.

"I think I might be falling in love with her," he allowed.

His father glowered. "You're not sure?"

"I've barely been back a few weeks. It's too soon to be sure."

"Everything doesn't need to be set in stone, does it? Just because you won't be living here don't mean you can't continue to write. Does it?"

"So you think I should go?"

"I think you should figure out what's stopping you. I refuse to think it's the change in your schedule, son." He paused. "Unless, of course, you had decided to leave the mission field."

"I can't do that." That was one thing he knew for sure. He loved his work.

"Then why does the timing matter so much?"

"I feel like I'm betraying you."

His father closed his eyes. "Edward, when your mother died, we both changed. That is the Lord's way. He guides us, makes us grow and change, even when we aren't ready. Edward, I am not the same man that I was when we lived in our little house."

"I don't think you're so different."

"Then you aren't seeing me, son. Please listen to me closely. I *wanted* to move here. I wanted to be around other people, I wanted to spend my days reading and playing cards and talking with people my age. You didn't stick me in a rest home. I *chose* to live here. That's the God's honest truth, no matter how guilty you might feel."

That was what he'd needed to hear. His father's no-nonsense way of talking. It sliced through his doubts and all the garbage he'd been carrying around.

"If I go, I'm really going to miss you."

"I will miss you, too. But this is how it's supposed to be, *boo*. I raised you to go out in the world, not to always stay by my side. I'm not ready for you to be at my beck and call. I don't want to be coddled and sat with. I want to read about your adventures and imagine your job. I want to sit by the fire and be proud of you because I know you are doing God's work. Most importantly, I want to feel at peace, because I know you are happy."

What could Ed say to that?

His *daed* scowled. "Now, you still have some figuring out to do. You go talk to Viola Keim and see if what you think you have is strong enough to last."

"There's also the dog," he continued in a rush. He'd completely forgotten about Gretta. "I've got a dachshund at home.

Her name is Gretta. I'm fond of her . . . I don't know what I'd do with her if I left. She just got settled at home. It seems cruel to take her to the pound."

"You're worried about a dachshund?"

"Kind of." But of course it wasn't really the dog. Gretta seemed to be a fitting symbol of the joy that he'd unexpectedly found in Berlin. He couldn't discount it.

And he didn't want to give it up without careful thought.

The lines around his father's eyes deepened. "Oh, for heaven's sakes, Edward, you worry too much."

"I like this dog."

"Well, it's certainly amazing to me that you get anything done in foreign countries without my prodding. If you decide to go to Belize, simply bring the dog here."

"They don't allow dogs here."

Deftly, his father ignored his protests. "Edward, is she house-trained?"

"Jah."

"Does she bite?"

"*Nee.* She's even-tempered."

"Does she run around a lot, chew on things?"

"No, she just wants to sit on her bed."

"If she only wants to sit around, then she's going to fit in here perfectly," he stated with a wry grin. "Bring the *hund* by, and I'll take care of her getting checked in." He folded his arms over his bony chest. "Next problem?"

"Um. Well, I don't have any."

"I should hope not!" With a grunt, his father got to his feet. "I for one can't think of another thing you need to worry about." Clapping his hands lightly he said, "Well, you'd best go off now and make your phone calls."

"What are you going to do?"

"I, son, am going back to bed. Organizing your life wears me out. Come back tomorrow and tell me what Viola said."

"I will." He stepped forward, reaching out to grip his father's arm. It was still thin and frail feeling. But now Ed realized that looks had been deceiving. Underneath the age spots and thin, papery skin was a strength Ed could only hope to one day possess. "Hey, Daed?"

"Hmm?"

"Danke."

"Anytime, Edward. Anytime at all." His

daed smiled slightly before tottering back to his room. Walking by himself.

Making Ed realize that it was time he did the same thing. It was time to make his own way in the world, even if his steps weren't as steady or as strong and sure as he wanted them to be.

Calling Mr. Cross was easier than Ed had imagined. Mr. Cross was glad to hear from Ed, and Ed was relieved to tell him that he was willing to go to Belize to begin setting up the mission.

The moment the words left his lips, he felt a fresh sense of peace.

"I'm thrilled, and I know the rest of the team will feel the same way," Mr. Cross said. "We knew you'd be perfect for the position. But if you get there and you change your mind, don't forget that you can still back out. You haven't made a firm commitment yet."

"I appreciate that. But I plan to accept, unless I truly feel like I couldn't do the work you are asking of me."

"Fair enough. I'll get on the computer and make plane and hotel reservations. I'll call later with the details."

"Sounds good." When they hung up, he looked at little Gretta who was curled up by his side. "I guess it's really happening." Now there was only one thing to do. Go visit Viola. Though he wasn't usually the type to consider traveling with a dog, he decided to take the dog in the buggy. Viola might go easier on him if he had Gretta by his side.

Thirty minutes later, he had the horse hitched to the buggy, and he was heading to the Keims' home. He hoped he would know the right words to say when he got there.

Right now? His brain felt suspiciously like mush. There was far too much to think about. And hope for.

Grinning broadly, Roman stuck his head in the kitchen door. "You've got a suitor, Viola."

Nearly dropping the plate she'd been washing, Viola gaped at her brother. "What are you talking about?"

"Edward Swartz is here, looking as impatient as I've ever seen a man." Clearing his throat, he added, "And . . . he brought his dog."

"What in the world?"

Her mother chuckled behind her.

Feeling her cheeks heat in embarrassment, she said, "Well, Roman, are you going to send him in?"

"He's coming. And, Mamm," he continued a little too sweetly, "Edward wants to know if he may bring his dog inside. What should I tell him?"

"I suppose you should tell him yes," her mother said. "My goodness, Viola. I've never heard of a man bringing his dachshund when courting."

Viola spun, wondering how she even knew about the dog when she saw that her mother was unabashedly watching Edward stride across the snowy yard to the front door.

"Oh, no," she moaned, glancing down at her stained dress and apron. She looked like she'd been doing exactly what she had been doing: washing dishes, polishing shelves, and wiping down baseboards. "Distract him or something, wouldja? I look awful."

"Go wash your face, dear. I can get the door," her mother offered just as Ed knocked.

"Better hurry, Twin," Elsie chirped from the chair in the back of the room where she'd been pairing socks. "Ed seems particularly anxious today."

"I'm hurrying!" She'd just closed the bathroom door when she heard the door open and her mother greet Edward. And the dog.

Edward had come calling! What was she going to tell him?

Oh, if only there were time to change into a dress that didn't smell like furniture polish! Quickly, she removed her kapp, washed her face, smoothed her hair, and then replaced her kapp. All in five minutes.

After scrambling back down the stairs, she found Edward and his dog sitting on one side of the room, her mother, Elsie, and her grandmother on the other. Neatly stacked in the middle of the table was a pile of roast beef sandwiches.

Her mother's lips curved in a self-satisfied way when she approached. "Viola, we were just feeding Edward, here."

"So I see."

He looked up at her and winked. "I'm a lonely bachelor. I never turn down food."

"You should have had him over for supper, Viola," her mother chided. "I had no idea you two had gotten so close."

Viola decided it wouldn't do any good to mention that until recently she hadn't even liked him. Instead, she sat down next to Elsie. "I guess you all have been catching up?"

"I did. And this is Gretta. I guess you could say she is the newest member of my family."

Looking at the dog, Viola couldn't help but be charmed by the dog's compact body. "She's adorable."

Looking pleased with the compliment, the little dog wagged her tail. Then she rocked back up on her haunches, obviously more eager to beg for scraps from Ed than to make new friends.

"He's been filling us in on his job," her mother said. "Mission work is commendable."

"Indeed," her grandmother added. "Though it's a shame that it takes you so far away from home."

"It's the nature of it, I'm afraid. We go to the people in need, not wait for them to come to us."

"But you enjoy your work?" Elsie asked.

"Yes. Very much so."

Her grandmother reached down and rubbed Gretta's head, who had nestled against her feet. "How did you two meet?"

"It was through his father. Mr. Swartz lives at Daybreak," Viola offered.

"Ah," her mother murmured. Giving a world of information in that statement.

Edward merely ate another bite of his sandwich.

"I like Mr. Swartz very much. He's one of my favorite residents," she added a little awkwardly. When Edward smiled at her, she stilled.

Then smiled back. Because she was realizing that she didn't want to be anywhere else.

Feeling awkward but happy, she was glad he'd come over. And glad, too, when a few minutes later, her sister, *mamm*, and grandmother left, leaving them alone. Taking her grandmother's seat, Viola was now close enough to pet Gretta . . . and spy the tiny gold flecks in Ed's blue eyes. "So, you decided to stop by."

"I did." His expression was more serious now. "I wanted to let you know that I decided to go to Belize next week."

"I thought you might," she said lightly, hoping her easy manner was camouflaging her disappointment. "It's an honor to be asked."

"It is an honor, but now it's starting to feel right, too," he said. "I can still change my mind, but I've decided that it would be wrong of me to refuse this."

She agreed with everything he said. But still it hurt. She was going to miss him—and miss what the two of them could have been. "I think you made the right decision."

"Do you?" His gaze was piercing. "Viola, I feel like we just found each other. I don't want to lose you."

His words were beautiful, but they scared her, too. It felt like it was all too much, too soon. "We don't have each other." She resented him assuming so much.

"Are you sure about that? I feel like we have a future."

"You do?"

"Well, I feel like we could have a future together. . . . Don't you feel the same way?"

Emotions warred inside her. She wanted

to believe what he said, to believe in him. She wanted to jump headfirst into a serious relationship, but what was happening was far from her comfort zone.

She was used to doing the pushing. Not being the one who got pushed!

"I'm not like you, Ed," she sputtered. "I can't make a decision like that so quickly."

"What more do you need?" His expression was honest, frank.

She needed him to want to stay. She wanted him to be different. And, perversely, she wanted him to stay exactly the same. She liked who he was. She admired his dedication. But she didn't know if that was enough. "I don't know. . . . Time, maybe? Ed, I do like you. But I like my family, too. I love them. I don't know if I could ever give up everything I know for the chance of happiness with you." She wanted to add her fears about Elsie, too—how she worried about leaving her, because she felt responsible for her twin. But Viola was afraid to say that out loud. No way did she want Elsie to overhear her saying such things.

"For the chance?" His voice was thick with sarcasm.

"I'm trying to be honest, Edward."

"I appreciate that. I do." He stood up then, his expression curiously flat. "Can I see you again before I go?"

"Of course. I mean, I'll probably see you at Daybreak."

"Oh. Sure."

Viola hated that she was hurting his feelings. But could he understand her side of things? "Edward, I don't know what you want me to do."

"I think you do. I'm asking you to take a leap of faith. I'm asking you to throw all your usual expectations of courting out the window and imagine us being together one day."

"Even if you are in Belize and I am not?"

"Even then."

"But what if one of us gets hurt?" A fresh wave of desperation flowed through her. She now knew that relationships could fall apart, even solid ones. Thinking of how upset her grandparents and parents had been lately, she knew she didn't want that kind of pain. "What if we both get hurt?"

"Then we'll hurt and we'll heal." He turned to the dog who was sitting at his feet. "Come along, Gretta."

After he left, she stared at the door. Had she just made the biggest mistake of her life? Tears pricked at her eyes. Oh, why couldn't something in her life be easy? Everywhere she turned, there seemed to be conflict and pain.

She started when she felt her mother's touch on her shoulder. "It will be all right, Viola. If it's meant to be, it will be."

"Are you sure?"

"*Nee.* But I'm hopeful."

Reaching up, she covered her mother's hand with her own. "Then I'm hopeful, too."

The next Monday, when she arrived at Daybreak, she found a note awaiting her.

Viola,

I'm leaving in the morning, but wanted to leave you a quick note. I'm excited about the trip, and am excited to figure out if Belize is the best place for my next mission. Please don't forget the things we talked about. I do care about you, and I do hope that one day we'll have a future together.

Please take care of yourself, don't work too hard, and don't let my father

always beat you at cards. He's getting
a little full of himself, I fear.
    Yours,
    Ed

Tears sprang to her eyes as she carefully folded the note. Ed's letter was so very much like him. Honest, but filled with humor, too. She was really going to miss him while he was on his trip.

But even more than that, she knew she was going to really miss him if he went to Belize for good.

chapter twenty-three

"Peter?" Marie murmured as she shook his shoulder. "You need to wake up and join us downstairs. Lorene is here with John."

Startled, he sat up in a rush, then had to close his eyes as the room spun. With effort, he opened his eyes and tried to focus. "Sorry, I guess I fell asleep."

Marie looked at him, her expression full of pain. "It's six o'clock."

She had a point. He'd never made a habit of napping. And if he had ever decided to lie down, it wouldn't have been so close to their regular bedtime. "I don't know what happened," he said. Of course, the moment he said the words he ached to take them back. He knew that he'd given in to temptation and had been drinking again.

Marie knew it, too.

Feeling even more despondent than usual, he got to his feet. By her look of dismay, he realized that he probably looked even more disheveled than he felt. Running a hand over his beard, he mumbled, "I guess I look a sight?"

She looked away. "Do you want to meet us in the kitchen?" her voice was flat. "Maybe you could wash up or something."

Or something. "Make me some coffee, will you? I'll be right there."

"All right."

After grabbing a fresh shirt, he walked to the bathroom and splashed some cold water on his face. Next he changed his shirt and brushed his hair.

Only then did he dare look at himself in the mirror.

Red eyes and a vacant look, full of regrets, stared back at him. He'd truly been a fool to think that he could beat his problem on his own. All he'd done was delay the inevitable.

By the time he got to the kitchen, it was

packed with family members wearing happy expressions. The girls and Roman were there, Sam and Mary Beth, too. His father stood by the stove, and looked pleased as punch. Even his mother was beaming, though she was standing a bit to the side, like an afterthought.

His mother cast a cool eye in his direction and raised a brow. Revealing all that she thought. It looked as if the only person he'd been fooling was himself.

"What is the happy occasion?" he asked. As if it wasn't obvious to them all.

"John and I spoke to the bishop this morning," Lorene said in a burst of smiles. "He agreed that we could marry in one month."

Marie fanned herself. "A wedding in one month? Lorene, couldn't we push it back?"

"*Nee,*" she said with a smile. "We have waited long enough. Besides, I don't need anything fancy."

"Plus, I already have a *haus*," John said.

"We won't be needing any gifts or money," Lorene added.

"And a simple meal of sandwiches would be fine," John added as he stepped a little bit closer to his bride-to-be. "All we really want is to exchange our vows. Finally, after all this time."

While Marie and Mary Beth exchanged exasperated glances, Viola and Elsie sighed at the romance of it all.

But then his mother's voice cut through the happy atmosphere. "Nonsense," she said.

The room went silent.

As Lorene looked like she was about to take John and leave for good, Peter tried to settle the room. "Mamm," he said sharply. "This is Lorene's day. We need to honor that. We'll make do."

"We will not simply be making do. This is my youngest *maydel*'s wedding, and we are hardworking, smart, and capable people. We'll do this right." Clapping her hands, she eyed Roman, Aaron, Peter, and John. "You men need to leave. Go sit in the parlor and talk or watch the fire or something. We women have things to do."

Viola laughed delightedly. "Mommi, you really think we can put on a proper wedding in one month, don'tcha?"

"There is no doubt in my mind that we can."

As Marie and Mary Beth started to smile,

relief poured through Peter. This excitement felt like a balm to the many sore feelings in the room.

Raising his voice, he said, "Men, you heard my mother. We're not needed here."

"Thank the good Lord," Sam said.

"Don't have to ask me twice," Roman added.

Only John Miller hesitated. "Will you be all right, Lorene?"

"Oh my goodness! She'll be fine, John," Mary Beth said. "Now, out you go."

As the men walked out, Lorene stared at her mother in surprise. At first she yearned to question her mother's sudden enthusiasm, but a sixth sense warned her to keep quiet. This, she realized, was her way of apologizing. Either Lorene could give in gracefully or pick a fight. Neither would undo the past ten years.

Thankfully, she was old and wise enough to choose the right path. "*Danke,* Mamm," she said simply.

"It's nothing." Her mother's smile was awkward and stilted. But present. "I, for one, think sometimes girls get too wrapped up in the busyness of planning a wedding. I'd rather do things like this. Quickly."

"Heaven knows it couldn't be any quicker," her sister-in-law Mary Beth murmured.

"Aunt Mary Beth!" Viola screeched. "I can't believe you said that."

"It's true," Lorene said with a shrug. "I'm eager to be John's *frau*. I can't deny it."

"I, uh, do believe I'll make us some coffee." Marie stood up, obviously a little frazzled.

Turning their way, Lovina said, "Elsie, you or your sister go find me a pencil and a notebook. We'll need to begin some lists."

Elsie immediately got to her feet, though Lorene noticed she smiled in her grandmother's direction. Then before another minute passed, she placed two pencils and a thick notebook in front of their matriarch.

Lovina picked up the pencil and tapped it experimentally on the paper before looking at the group of them. "There's only one thing to do in an instance like this," she announced.

"And what is that?" Lorene asked.

"We're going to need to make decisions fast, then split up. Lorene, will 7UP Chicken do?"

"Of course."

"What about mashed potatoes, corn, and peas? Stuffing and salad?"

"Those will be fine," she replied. Realizing, as they all did, that her mother had just named the traditional meal of any wedding luncheon.

"And date-nut pudding? And cake, too?"

"Yes to all of it," she said with a smile.

"Colors?"

"Lovina, I don't think we'll need to worry about that. . . ."

"Nonsense, Marie. I can still sew a dress in a day. If I'm not cooking, I'll be able to make everyone's dress with Viola's help." She arched an eyebrow in Viola's direction.

Lorene half expected Viola to balk at the sudden job. After all, she had a job at Daybreak. But she merely nodded solemnly. "*Jah,* Mommi. I can help you sew as much as you want."

"*Gut.*" She tapped her pencil again. "Make a decision, and be quick about it, Lorene. You've waited long enough for this day. Surely you've had something in mind during all this time?"

Oh, but her mother could make paint wish itself away! "I've always fancied pink," she admitted, feeling a little self-conscious.

The room fell silent, and she blushed to the roots of her hair as she realized that to everyone else she was a thirty-two-year-old spinster. She was long past the age of pink dresses.

Her mother cleared her throat and looked at her until Lorene could stand it no more and met her gaze. "I think pink is a *gut* choice, Lorene."

"I do, too," Marie said with an understanding smile. "And pink will look lovely on everyone."

Lorene felt her eyes prick with tears of happiness. Finally, she was planning her wedding day. Finally, she was sitting with women that she loved, and she was the focus of the blushes and giggles of amusement.

It was embarrassing and prideful and lovely. It was everything she'd given up on.

"Lorene?" John's voice said from the doorway. "Lorene, are you crying? Is anything wrong?"

As Elsie handed her a tissue, she smiled at John. "Don't you worry, John Miller. Your Lorene is just fine."

"Then why is she crying?"

"Because she's happy, of course," Elsie

declared. Just as the other women laughed and John's eyes widened.

They all heard the other men teasing him, loudly and boisterously. "That's what you get for going in there, man!"

The women around her giggled as Marie placed a cup of coffee to her right. "You go ahead and cry, dear. After all, this moment only happens once."

Lorene knew that to be true.

Late that night, Elsie rolled over on her side and whispered in the dark, "Viola, are you awake?"

"Uh-huh." She'd spent the last hour sitting in the dark, hoping for sleep but knowing it wasn't going to come anytime soon. All she could seem to do was think about Ed in Belize and wonder how his trip was going . . . all while doing her best to not miss him so much.

It had been an impossible task.

"Tonight was *wunderbaar*, don'tcha think?"

"It was."

Elsie's voice turned dreamy. "I know Aunt Lorene is wishing all this had happened years ago, but her marrying John on the spur of the moment is sure romantic, ain't so?"

"Jah." It had been romantic, the way Lorene had looked so in love and how John looked like he could hardly stand to be away from her. The whole family had hardly been able to keep their eyes off the pair, not even their grandmother. More than once Viola had seen her grandmother's expression soften as she looked at Lorene.

And it had been so sweet of her to offer to sew all the dresses. Viola hadn't even minded being recruited in the project without being asked.

Of course, if the night had been so wonderful, why had she felt like crying every time she saw Lorene and John together?

Why did she feel like crying now?

As if in answer, tears appeared in her eyes. Rolling onto her back, she swiped at her eyes.

"Viola, what if that never happens to us?" Elsie's voice was hesitant.

"You mean marriage?" To be honest, she'd never imagined Elsie ever getting married. With her sister's eyesight getting worse with each year, Viola had always assumed that they'd all take care of her.

That she'd live with either her or Roman or even her parents.

"Of course, marriage."

"Well, I am sure we'll find the right men. Eventually."

"Haven't you already found him?"

"You mean Edward?"

"Of course." Impatience pierced her tone. "Come now, Viola. You aren't living in a closed box. We've all been watching, and we all reckon you've fallen in *lieb*. I mean, you have, haven't you?"

Well, she wasn't sure. She'd always expected love to feel warmer, safer. Instead, she felt like she was perched on the edge of a cliff, and she was holding on tightly to her past because the future seemed far too scary.

However, Edward did make her feel more alive. When she was around him, she felt as if every nerve had been awakened. Like she'd suddenly begun a brand-new day, and the past, the rest of her life before him, had been spent asleep.

"Hey . . . Viola?"

"I'm still awake."

"Well? What is happening with you and Edward?"

"Nothing. He's in Belize."

"I know that."

"Well, you don't know everything, Twin." Swallowing hard, she added, "He was asked to be the head of the mission there. If he accepts the job, he'll be gone for five years."

"That's a mighty long time to be apart."

"It feels like a lifetime."

After a moment, Elsie said, "But you could go, right?"

"Me? In Belize?" She laughed softly. "What would I do there?"

"You'd be Ed's wife, of course."

"I'd be far away, Elsie. I couldn't come home whenever I needed to."

"But you'd already be home, right?"

Viola propped herself up on her elbows. "Do you hear what you're saying?"

"I'm saying that if you married him and moved away, you'd be growing up, and moving on."

Elsie always was too practical. "No, I wouldn't be growing up and moving on. I'd be leaving my job and my family and everything I ever knew. I'd be foolish." Plus, who would look out for Elsie if she was gone?

Pure silence met her declaration.

Now it was Viola who was calling out her sister's name. "Elsie?"

"Sorry. Ah, yes. I suppose you have a point."

"I know I do." Feeling more confident, she added, "Twin, your problem is that you're getting swept away by the romance of it all. But in the light of day, a woman must be able to look at her man and her life and know that she made the right decision."

When Elsie didn't reply, Viola flopped over on her side and stared at the blank wall. And tried to find comfort in knowing that for the foreseeable future, this would be her room, and her bed, and what she would see when she went to sleep for the next year.

And she tried to find comfort in that.

She tried to find any comfort in it at all.

chapter twenty-four

When Mr. Cross met him at baggage claim in Columbus, Ed was so exhausted from the trip, he was really glad to see a familiar face. "Thank you for picking me up."

"It was no problem," the CAMA director said, looking especially pleased. "Actually, I heard such good reports about your visit, I was anxious to hear news firsthand."

Ed was eager to share news from his trip. From the moment he'd arrived in the country, he'd felt as if the Lord had been with him. The residents of the area had been open and helpful, and there wasn't any of the lingering sense of danger that had always felt present in Nicaragua. Instead, he'd felt called to the villages that they visited, and had felt accepted and wanted by the villagers.

But how did he put such feelings into words? He needed to relay facts and statistics, not warm feelings and emotions.

As he grabbed his duffel bag, he said, "The building CAMA purchased is in good condition. There's quite a bit of room. We should be able to house six or seven people easily, as well as a large assortment of supplies."

Mr. Cross nodded as they walked out the automatic sliding door and into the parking garage. "Good. That's good."

The temperature hovered near freezing. Ed shivered. Already his body had acclimated itself to the warmer climate. He'd taken his body's ability to accept the humidity and warm temperatures easily as yet another sign that moving to Belize was the right choice.

After they got in his truck and the heat was blasting, Mr. Cross turned to him. "Are you hungry? We can stop somewhere, or even go through a drive-thru before we hit the road back to Berlin."

"I am hungry. But I don't care where we go."

"There's a Wendy's up here. How about we get that?"

"That works for me."

Ed ate while his boss followed the car's navigational system to get onto Highway 62.

By the time they were on the road, Ed had wolfed down his burger, and he had a better idea of what to report. "There was real interest in our bundle project, and in our food and clothing programs. I found a few people who have a real relationship with Christ who want to make the mission a success." He continued some more, discussing his ideas for growth, his targeted plans for the next year, as well as some personal reflections.

Even he heard the excitement in his voice as they zipped toward home. In many ways, his mind was still on the island.

"You've done an amazing amount of work in a short amount of time, Ed," Mr. Cross said as he continued down the windy two-laned highway toward Berlin. "I know the people you serve will be in good hands when you return. God has blessed us all."

That caught him off guard. He'd only committed to going on this short trip—not accepting the five-year commitment. He thought he was clear that he needed to make sure the calling felt right. And while part of him wanted to accept without reservations, he still wasn't a hundred percent sure that he was ready to head up the Belize office. Not yet. Not until he talked to Viola and his father again. "I still need to do some thinking about this," he said.

"Truly? You sounded so enthused about Belize on the phone. We were sure it was a perfect placement for you."

It did feel perfect, so much so that Ed had felt as if the Lord really did want him to head to Belize. But before he'd been asked to go, he'd begun to feel at home in Berlin all over again. "It was a good fit, but I still need to pray about this. And to talk to some people who are important to me."

"Your father?"

"Yes. And, well, there's a woman, too."

"Ah." The lines around his mouth softened. "I didn't know you had someone special in your life, Ed."

"It's kind of a sudden thing."

"I'm sure you know that we have several

married missionaries in the field. Of course, we'd pay for your wife's traveling expenses, too. We want you to be able to concentrate on your job, not be missing her."

"We haven't gotten that far." As he glanced out the window, watching the fields and farmhouses pass by, he wondered what it was going to take to convince Viola to take a chance on them.

No, that wasn't what he wanted. He wanted her to believe in them so much that she couldn't imagine another life but one by his side.

How did that happen?

"I see." Mr. Cross's voice was deflated. "Ed, I don't need to tell you that people's lives are at stake. I need you to be completely on board with this plan."

"I know. And I will be. I just need a few days to finalize my decision. And to talk to Viola."

"I hope that's all it will take."

Ed didn't care for the criticism he heard in his boss's voice. "Two weeks ago, I was looking forward to several months of reconnecting with my father and getting acclimated in my home. Now you are expecting me to change everything I'd planned on in a matter of days. I understand the urgency, but I'm asking you to understand that I will only be able to go if I feel it is the only right decision. If I'm torn, I won't be any good for anyone."

"You're right, of course. But Edward, as much as I'd like to give you all the time you need, the fact of the matter is I simply cannot."

"I understand. I promise, I'll do my best to make a decision soon."

Mr. Cross nodded, but the friendly, celebratory mood in his vehicle turned to a strained silence.

Ed began counting the minutes until he was home.

The next morning, Ed still felt exhausted. When he arrived at Daybreak, he greeted Nancy, put his coat and hat in the cloakroom, then walked toward the back parlor. As he got closer, Ed found himself listening for his father's voice, for the laughter that seemed to be so much a part of his life here.

And sure enough, as he turned the corner and was just steps away from the parlor, he heard his father, Mr. Showalter, and

Viola Keim all having another one of their silly arguments.

He faltered, rethinking his timing. Was he ready to announce his news to everyone at the same time?

But of course, it wasn't like he had a choice. Everyone was going to be curious.

Bracing himself, he walked through the doorway and kept a smile on his face as his two favorite people in the world stopped abruptly and stared at him.

"You're back," his *daed* murmured.

"I got home last night. I was going to call you, call both of you this morning, but decided it would be better to see you in person."

His father held out a hand. Ed clasped it, then gently enfolded his dad in his arms, hugging him tightly. "Daed, are you feeling better?"

His father patted his back, then pushed him away so they could see each other's face. "I'm fine. As I told you, it was just a cold."

He couldn't go another moment without meeting Viola's gaze. "I'm glad you are here, too."

She took a seat.

He could have sworn her hands were shaking, but he could have very well misjudged that. "How are you, Viola?"

"I'm well." Scooting closer, she said, "Don't keep us in suspense, Edward. Tell us about Belize."

He drew a deep breath, wondering where to start. "Well, first off, it is very beautiful." Slowly, he began to talk about the island, and the hills, and the people there. He told them about the small Amish and Mennonite population of hardy farmers. They'd begun to settle in the area around 2006 and had quickly become a respected community in the area.

He talked, too, of the many poor communities who were struggling with fresh water and proper sanitation.

Both Viola and his father looked like they were hanging on every word. He couldn't tell if they were truly interested or whether they were waiting for him to tell them his decision.

He told them about the mission house, and the plans to make a more substantial compound. He told them about the heat and the flowers the women had given him with tears in their eyes, knowing that CAMA was determined to help their plight.

"Edward, it sounds like quite a trip," his father said when he finished.

"Yes. Yes, it was."

"Do you know when you're going back? Do you have a date?"

"Nee."

"Mr. Cross didn't give you a date? I must say I'm surprised."

"It's not that. I didn't tell him that my mind was made up."

His father scowled. "But, Edward, we talked. I don't want you staying here for me."

Looking at Viola, he murmured, "Daed, I love you. But this time I wasn't thinking about you."

Looking from Ed to Viola, his father slowly smiled. "I see. Well, then. It seems to me that the two of you have some talking to do."

"When do you get off work?" Ed asked, unable to look away.

"At noon."

"Can I come see you then? Maybe we could go somewhere and talk?"

"Yes . . . that sounds *gut*." She smiled, then with a mumble about other work to do, she scampered out of the room.

From the corner, Mr. Showalter chuckled. "I swear, Edward, watching you is better than any soap opera I've ever seen on television. You've got more going on than a band of neighborhood housewives."

He laughed at the description. "It feels like it, for sure."

"Do you know what you want to do, Ed?" his father asked.

"I want to make Viola happy," he said slowly, letting his heart speak for him instead of overthinking it all. "Until right this minute, I thought that there was only Belize for me. But that isn't true. Before I came home, I couldn't imagine serving anywhere besides Nicaragua. Now God has shown me the error of that thought. If Viola isn't ready for me to leave, then I'll tell Mr. Cross no and wait for the next opportunity."

"That sounds like a wise choice."

"No," Mr. Showalter said with a wry grin. "It sounds like your boy is in love. With our favorite girl! Now who would of thought this would happen?"

His *daed* stretched and a self-satisfied smile, much like a Cheshire cat, lit his face. "Maybe one of us thought this might happen."

Crossing one foot over the opposite knee, Ed leaned back and grinned at his father. "Want to play cards?"

"I do. Are you prepared to lose?"

"I'm prepared for anything."

chapter twenty-five

In a panic, Viola practically ran to the staff lounge's phone. The moment her aunt picked up, she heaved a sigh of relief. "Thank goodness."

"Viola? Are you all right?"

"I think so."

"You think?"

There was nothing to do but blurt her news. "Aunt Lorene, Edward came back and he hasn't made a decision about his trip. I need your advice."

"You sure it's my advice that you need?" Her voice sounded amused. And a bit concerned, too.

"Of course. Aunt Lorene, what should I do? Should I tell him to go to Belize without me? Should I tell him that I want him to stay? Should I tell him that it's over between us, or that I simply need more time?"

"I can't tell you what to do, of course."

"But you must have an opinion."

"I truly don't, Viola. It's not for me to decide what Edward should do. Just as it isn't for me to tell you what you should do with him."

"But I'm going to see him at noon. I need to know something!"

"You need to stop trying to figure it all out ahead of time," she said quietly. "God will let you know what to do."

"But what about all the problems at home? What about Grandma? And Daed? And Elsie?" Panicked, she said, "If I don't look after Elsie, who will?"

"Viola, they are our family. We all love them, and they love us. But you can't live your life on the fringes of everyone else's. You have to accept that we each have our own path to follow."

"So you think I should go with him?"

"I didn't say that. Stop and take a deep

breath. Stop and let your wishes and the Lord's wishes shine through."

Viola closed her eyes in frustration. Why was every person in her life not giving her what she wanted?

"But, Lorene, I don't want to make the wrong decision."

"Take it from someone who did make a wrong decision many years ago. Even if you are wrong, things can change. Put down the phone, take a deep breath, and imagine your future. Imagine your life the way you want it. Then, Viola, close your eyes and find out who you see."

Moments later, Viola put down the phone and slowly walked back to the storage room, where she was supposed to unpack new boxes of supplies and organize files.

And in the silence of the room, she did what her aunt advised. She emptied her mind of all the issues and problems that she thought she'd had to shoulder. And instead, she let her heart guide her. "*Got*, what do you see? What should I see?" she whispered.

Closing her eyes tight, she waited for a picture to appear.

But nothing happened.

"God, I'm right here, waiting. If you could, please let me know your decision." Closing her eyes, she tried again. But yet again, nothing.

Frustrated, she felt her heartbeat quicken as frustration overtook her. Then, not knowing what else to do, she tore open a cardboard box and started unpacking a supply of paper goods. Feeling like a puppet on a string, she dug into the box and mechanically started lining up the boxes of tissue and rolls of toilet paper.

It was hard to believe she was doing such mundane things while trying to determine her future.

But then, as she was taking hold of a box of bandages and placing them in a cabinet, she felt the gentle nudging of the Lord's will. Suddenly, she was gripped by a picture of her future, and she knew without a doubt that the vision she was seeing was everything right and true.

All she'd had to do was have faith.

"Viola, it's sunny out," Ed announced. "A perfect day for a walk."

She turned his way and smiled. While the temperature was only in the thirties, it was an above-average day for winter in Ohio. The sky was a bright blue. Vibrant and breathtaking.

He continued, "I thought I might go home, get Gretta, and bring her back here. Would you like to walk with me?"

She nodded as she looked at him. He seemed to be holding himself a bit awkward and stiff, as if he was afraid of saying the wrong thing. She almost laughed, she knew the feeling so well.

As they walked along the sidewalk toward his home, Ed looked like he wanted to start several conversations, but was stopping himself. After a bit, he seemed to give up. Looking miserable, he bit his lip.

Viola didn't want to rush him or put words into his mouth. All her life, she'd been a bit too impulsive, a bit too outspoken. Today the Lord had shown her that she'd been wrong to push others and herself so much. So she was determined to hold her tongue.

When they got to his house, little Gretta greeted him exuberantly. Before he'd left, Ed had asked a few of the neighbors if one of them would mind looking out for his new pet. To his surprise, they'd all wanted to help care for the dog. His next-door neighbors had even volunteered to drop her off at the house about an hour ago.

Racing in a circle around him, the dog wagged her tail and barked happily. Kneeling on the wood floor, Edward looked just as pleased to see her.

Watching the two of them together, Viola felt the last bit of her worries fall away. Edward Swartz was a loving man, a giving man. A good man.

After a moment, Ed sat on the floor. Stretching his legs out in front of him, he looked up at her. "Viola, I feel so torn up inside, I've been really struggling with what to do."

Glad he was at last sharing his thoughts, she knelt down beside him. "I've felt much the same way."

"I love my life. I love this little dog. I want to be close to my father. But I want other things, too. What's more, I feel certain that the Lord wants to use me for mission work."

"I understand." Finally, she really did.

His eyes popped open, the blue of his irises making her breath catch. "Do you?" Before she could reassure him again, he rushed forward. "I suppose you think I'm the biggest jerk in the world, talking about missing the dog and not mentioning you."

"I don't think you're a jerk. But, what are you thinking?"

He looked at her, worry and concern bright in his gaze. Then, as if he couldn't take it anymore, he spoke. "If you want to know the truth, the reason I haven't been thinking about missing you is because I want you to come with me. I want you beside me, Viola. No matter what country I'm in. I feel called to be more than myself, and I feel like I can be that person. But only if you are there with me."

"Do you really think I can help that much?"

"I know you can help me. Viola, I know I'm asking a lot. Maybe even too much. But do you ever see a future where you could put me before the rest of your family? Where you could put an uncertain future of living in crazy conditions ahead of security and everything you've ever known?"

Just recently, she'd told him she couldn't. She'd been afraid to imagine a world where she wasn't sure of her place in it.

But now she understood she'd been

selfish. Even though she'd thought she'd been putting the other members of her family first, she'd actually been only thinking about herself. She had a vague sense that even her worries about Elsie's care had stemmed from her own need to look after her sister. Never had Elsie asked to be taken care of.

"Edward, I do think I can imagine a future like the one you're describing."

"You can?"

Oh, but there was such hope in his blue eyes! And because of that hope, she felt like she could admit what was in her heart. "Yes, because I've fallen in love with you."

"I love you, too," he said in a rush. "I want us to marry and for you to join me in Belize." He paused. "I mean, as soon as you are ready."

His excitement made her excited, too. But she still wanted to take things a bit more slowly.

"I have an idea. How about we plan for me to go with you, but in six months' time? We could write and call in the meantime. And I could even go out to visit you. But this way, I'd also have time to come to terms with all the changes that are happening. Then you could come here and we could get married, and then go out together."

"You'd be willing to do that?"

"I'd be willing to do just about anything, Edward. Except give you up."

Before she could brace herself, he'd wrapped his arms around her and pulled her close. Their awkward embrace caused them both to lose their balance. They toppled over in a jumble of arms and legs and laughter. Obviously confused, Gretta barked at them.

But Viola didn't care. Because Ed was holding her and laughing and kissing her and it felt right.

It felt right to be so free and open and loved. In fact, little had felt better.

"Bishop Coblentz gave me a name of a treatment facility," Peter told Marie with only the slightest tremor in his voice. "The bishop even called them while I was in his office. They have space available, so I'm going to go there this afternoon."

Marie reached out a hand. When he took it, feeling the fine bones under her soft, cool skin, he almost cried like a child.

How could he have come so close to jeopardizing everything they had?

"Would you like me to accompany you?"

He would've loved that. He would've loved to depend on her for a little while longer.

But it was time that he stood on his own.

"*Nee,* Marie. It's a program where you live there for a few weeks. I won't be coming home right away."

Her eyes widened. "Peter, truly?"

"There's more wrong than just drinking, Marie. Though I feel weak for admitting it, I've been having quite a time dealing with some things. I need to discover why that is. And more importantly, I need to get better, and once again become the man you can depend on. The man you married. Because, you know, we have so much that is right."

Slowly she nodded. "What can I help you with?"

She'd already helped him with so much. She'd seen him at his worst, and still stayed by his side. Now she was supporting him even though he was going to have to leave her for several weeks.

Asking her for one more thing seemed

like too much to ask, so he kept it simple. "Could you make me a sandwich? I need to go pack."

"*Jah,*" she replied, her voice wobbly. "*Jah, I can do that.*"

Later, he talked to Roman and the girls. It was hard, admitting his faults, but he figured they'd already witnessed him at his neediest. "I need you all to help with the extra chores out in the barn. Ask your uncle Sam or even John Miller if you need anything. They'd both be glad to help, so don't be shy if you're needing extra hands."

"I'll take care of things, Daed," Roman said solemnly. "Don't worry."

Looking into his son's eyes, Peter realized that his boy was all grown up. "*Danke,* Roman."

Next, he walked to the *dawdi haus* and told his mother and father his plans. Their expressions were solemn, but surprisingly, they only added their support.

Then all too soon, the English driver arrived and he hugged Marie goodbye.

"Will you call soon?" she asked as she raised her arms around his neck and pressed her face into his shoulder. Just the way she'd hugged him the first time.

Just like she had for over twenty years.

"I'll call when I can. But if you don't hear from me, don't assume the worst. I'll have to follow their rules for a time, and the bishop said that the treatment center can be fairly strict."

"I'll be praying for you, Peter."

He knew she would. And knowing that both she and the Lord were on his side? Well, that meant the world to him.

"That is what I need the most, Marie," he said sincerely.

She hugged him again and was still standing there, watching him leave when the car turned and sped up onto Highway 35. He was finally doing something right.

And after far too many weeks of feeling like he was doing too much wrong, it felt good indeed.

chapter twenty-six

"I still canna believe it, Lovina," Aaron said, his voice heavy with disappointment. "I can't believe Peter left the farm to go get help from some recovery clinic down near Columbus. I never thought I'd see the day."

"I never thought I would, either," Lovina murmured. But privately she was proud of her son.

What he was doing wasn't easy. Change never was.

Instead of dwelling on Peter, she looked out the window. It was still dark outside, but if she squinted, she could see the first rays of the sun glimmer over the horizon.

Just like the night before, her husband's voice sounded aggrieved. "I'm going to go to the barn to see if Roman needs any help. He probably doesn't, but I figure he's feeling a bit at a loss, now that his *daed* is off helping himself."

He'd paused expectantly. Obviously hoping for her to heap on the criticism. For most of their married lives, that had been their way.

But she was tired of that pattern.

So instead, she concentrated on the positive. It was easier, she thought. And besides, the sun was about to come up. "I think that's a *gut* idea, Aaron. Roman will appreciate your help for sure."

She felt him pause at the door, obviously waiting for her to turn around, but she didn't feel up to facing him. The emotions churning inside her were too strong. Too tumultuous.

"Lovina, did you hear about Viola? She said yes to that Edward Swartz."

"*Jah,* I heard." Still looking out the window, she smiled. That granddaughter of hers was certainly determined to follow her own path!

"Before we know it, she'll be leaving us.

Marie said they're going to let her go to Belize when she's married. Aren't you surprised she didn't put her foot down?"

She wasn't. But she thought Marie was far smarter than Lovina had ever been. After all, all putting her foot down had done was create a chasm between her and Lorene and postpone the inevitable. "It is God's will, I think," she said faintly.

"I'm not so sure I believe that."

"It's not like we have a choice. Viola is a grown woman."

Ah, there was the sun, illuminating the fields in the distance, just as if the first lights from heaven were reaching out to her in their wondrous glory.

With a grunt of exasperation, her husband walked away. She heard his boots pound along the wood floor she'd so carefully mopped yesterday. Never had he learned to take off his boots when he entered the house. Never in forty years.

She wondered why.

When the kitchen door closed and she was alone, she slowly rested her forehead on the cool pane of glass. The icy glass eased her worries, bypassing the mixed-up feelings of anger and betrayal she'd clung to for years.

Years!

Instead, with the cool glass against her skin and the growing light of the new morning shining in the distance, she felt acceptance.

Sometime between Peter finding her picture and Viola announcing that she was engaged to Edward Swartz and intended to go to Belize with him in six months time, Lovina knew she'd changed.

At sixty-four years of age, she'd finally decided to turn over a new leaf. She'd re-awakened.

When she'd been sure she'd lost everything, she cast off her worries and stopped living in fear of failure. Instead, she'd dared to accept herself, and more than that, accept her imperfections.

Her forehead had gotten chilled. Leaning back, she thought of her marriage, and of her past, and of her children and grandchildren.

She thought of her home, and of past disappointments. She thought of when her children were born, and about making dresses for Sara and Lorene and Elsie and Viola.

About making dresses for Lorene's wedding.

That's when she knew the truth. Life wasn't meant to be perfect. Instead, it was a series of glorious imperfections, made better by the promise of each new day. While every night could bring regrets and disappointments, each morning the sun rose again.

All she had to do was stand up and greet the shining rays of light. And celebrate that no matter what happened, those early-morning hours were a gift, a bounty. A miracle.

It was daybreak. The moment when everything was right in the world. Simply because they were alive. Simply because they were alive to share it.

Watching the sun rise, she gave thanks. After sixty-four years, she'd finally learned to be in awe of God's power . . . and the miracle of a brand-new day.

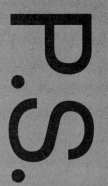

About the author

About the book

Insights,
Interviews &
More . . .

Meet Shelley Shepard Gray

I GREW UP IN HOUSTON, TEXAS, went to Colorado for college, and after living in Arizona, Dallas, and Denver, we moved to southern Ohio about ten years ago.

I've always thought of myself as a very hard worker, but not "great" at anything. I've obtained a bachelor's and master's degree . . . but I never was a gifted student. I took years of ballet and dance, but I was never anywhere near the star of any recital. I love to cook, but I'm certainly not close to being gourmet. And finally, I love to write books, but I've certainly read far better authors.

Maybe you are a little bit like me. I've been married for almost twenty years and have raised two kids. I try to exercise but really should put on my tennis shoes a whole lot more. I'm not a great housekeeper, I hate to drive in the snow, and I don't think I've ever won a Monopoly game. However, I am the best wife and mother I know how to be.

Isn't it wonderful to know that in God's eyes that is okay? That from His point of view, we are all exceptional? I treasure that knowledge and am always so thankful for my faith. His faith in me makes me stand a little straighter, smile a little bit more, and be so very grateful for every gift He's given me.

I started writing about the Amish because their way of life appealed to me. I wanted to write stories about regular, likable people in extraordinary situations—and who just happened to be Amish.

Getting the opportunity to write inspirational novels is truly gratifying. With every book, I feel my faith grows stronger. And that makes me feel very special indeed. ∾

Letter from the Author

Dear Reader,

What a year 2011 was for me. *The Protector* made the *New York Times* bestseller list! *The Survivor* made the *USA Today* bestseller list! My youngest child graduated from high school! What else happened? I had to go to the hospital for a sudden surgery. My mother-in-law was in intensive care for two straight weeks. Then my beautiful sister-in-law died. So did my mother. So did our fifteen-year-old beagle—the only dog my kids had ever had.

It was definitely one of the more difficult years of my family's life. Every month, when my husband and I met with our small group at church, we'd take a breath before beginning our prayer requests. We had so many.

I guess all of these unexpected events had a lot to do with the writing of this book. I vividly recall exactly where I was when Meagan from Harper

Collins called to tell me about the *New York Times* list. And when my brother called to tell me about my mother's passing.

Sometimes a two-minute conversation really can change your life.

I hope you enjoyed getting to know the Keim family of Berlin, Ohio. Their complicated love for each other feels very real to me. I've also especially enjoyed the chance to return to Holmes County. I love the rolling hills, the quaint streets and shops. I love the sense of peace I feel whenever I return . . . and most of all, the many people I've met there.

The next book in the Days of Redemption series is *Ray of Light.* In it, Roman Keim is forced to choose to either become more involved in the complicated problems his family is facing . . . or to walk away from it all for a lovely woman he meets in the Amish community of Pinecraft, Florida.

Until then, I hope to see you on Facebook, on my website's

blog . . . or maybe even at one of the many book signings and appearances I have planned. Thank you for reading my books and for telling your friends and family about them, too. God bless you all.

With my blessings,
Shelley Shepard Gray

Shelley Shepard Gray
10663 Loveland,
Madeira Rd. #167,
Loveland, OH 45140

Questions for Discussion

1. The inspiration for *Daybreak* came from the song "Closer to Love" by Mat Kearney. There's a line in it that spoke to me: "I guess we're all one phone call from our knees." Have you ever had a moment in your life when an unexpected phone call, email, or letter brought you to your knees?

2. I couldn't really fault Viola for not understanding Ed's need to do mission work in foreign countries—she'd never been out of Holmes County, Ohio. Where is the farthest that you've traveled? How has that experience changed your perspective about other places? About your own hometown?

3. Peter's dependency on alcohol was difficult to write about. However, I wanted to add his storyline after reading an ad in *The Budget* for an alcohol and drug treatment center catering to

the Amish and Mennonites. It showed me that no single group of people is completely immune to addictions. Why do you think that is? How would this kind of addiction be different in a community like the Amish?

4. How would Atle Swartz's life have been different if he'd never gone to Daybreak Retirement Home? If Ed had never left Berlin?

5. If Lovina had been open about her past, do you think her children would have chosen different paths? What might have changed?

6. Have you ever gone on a mission with your church or another community group? How has the experience influenced you?

7. Ed feels that God meant for him to work in the mission field. I've often felt that God meant for me to write. What gifts has the Lord given you that were meant to be used for His glory?

8. I really enjoyed writing about Lorene and John's romance. What do you think would have happened to them if they'd gotten together ten years ago? How can something be sweeter when you have to wait for it?